Auctioning Off Existence

Auctioning Off Existence

The Tragedy of the Amazon Rainforest

Aashay Mody

Cover art and design by Dreamink Studio
Author photo by Aashay Mody

An effort has been made to provide as accurate scientific information as possible, however, due to the fictional nature of this work, certain exceptions have been made for the sake of the story.

ISBN 979-8-218-16776-9

Aashay Mody
Contact at aashaymodybooks@gmail.com

Prologue

Silver rays of moonlight spread across the Amazon Rainforest, giving it an air of mystery as they reflected off the water and made ancient ruins glow amid the chirping of insects and occasional splashes of water from small fish. Ripples unfurled across the surface of the river when branches snapped and fell from above. Two dazzling green eyes blinked from the undergrowth, revealing the mighty presence of a jaguar. The cat slinked toward the water, moving his shoulders up and down as he walked. His golden fur, dappled with rosettes, hid his body in the shadows and made his carriage all the more awe-inspiring. Smaller animals resting on the riverbank scurried away, cowering beneath his lethal elegance, but, tonight, he was only looking for a drink. Lapping the water up with his tongue, the jaguar shook his fur in the wind, sending droplets cascading into the trees. Turning around, he walked up a low tree, stretched his jaw, and settled down to sleep.

Chapter 1

An ocelot awoke to high-pitched screeching that came from the animal who dared rest upon his fur and pull his ears. He bared his teeth and growled in rage, succeeding in scaring a young monkey who jumped from his back to the branches in front of him. It would have taken the slightest movement for the ocelot to ensnare the primate's leg in his jaws, but he was young once too. And just as foolish. In any case, the retaliation from the other monkeys would be too much of a nuisance.

More shrieking came from the trees above as the young monkey's troop sounded an alarm call and beckoned the monkey away. She scampered up the tree chattering unintelligibly and followed her mother as the troop swung through the treetops toward the edge of their territory to bask in the morning sun. The monkeys' thick black fur became shiny and smooth as they rested and gorged upon sweet fruits and leaves. Even after her mother had chided her for going near the ocelot, the young monkey's adventurous spirit had not been extinguished and she was now competing with other young ones to see who could climb the highest. Ever so often, one did fall and hit their head on the ground, but the high risk made the younglings' exploits fun.

The young monkey ventured quite far and found her way into a macaw's nest, grabbing an egg and shaking the newfound object. The parents furiously cawed and batted their wings until the monkey had to let go.

The older monkeys called the other younglings down from the branches, but the young monkey relentlessly climbed on, taking in new sights, sounds, and smells. Her mother began to climb up after her and she went even further until she caught sight of a shiny object.

Leaping from branch to branch, then on to the new thing, the monkey began exploring every nook and cranny of the unknown discovery. But it was a metal machine, a large crane, and the humans in possession of it did not like tiny, grabby hands on their belongings.

"Hey," one of them called, "there's some tiny monkey thing on the crane."

"I'll take care of it," the man piloting the crane replied.

Soon the young monkey's mother had reached her baby and picked her up by the scruff of her neck. Just in time, the mother dropped her child onto a tree trunk when the crane rumbled and took the mother high in the air before sending her flying to the ground, breaking her neck in a clean snap.

The monkeys huddled together, waiting for the threat to pass, as the young monkey looked on in horror and sadness, unable to take in what had occurred.

Under cover of darkness, the troop recovered the mother's body and wept together. But the sound of the crane starting, paired with a bright flash of light, made all eyes turn toward the approaching machine. Except for the young monkey, who was on her knees, head bowed. The troop took to the trees amidst the commotion, leaving her in solitude. Although she had lots more to learn about the jungle, the young monkey vowed never to make the mistake again and locked off her curiosity, making her heart a cold, dark place. No longer would she rekindle that spark of adventure and be the cause of another death.

***

Water shot up from the river dolphin's fins as he raced down the Amazon River, ducking in and out of it, laughing at the surprised expressions of the ever-so-expressionless fish. His sister was right alongside him, darting and spiraling like a torpedo. The two were very close, best friends for as long as they remembered, and did everything together. He flicked up his tail and jumped out of the water, sending a catfish flying up and into his mouth.

His sister whistled disapprovingly, telling him that their parents didn't like when he ate catfish and reminding him of their uncle's tragic death.

He knew it wasn't the fish, though. It was the humans and their mining. Their endless greed for luxury items like the metallic sun-colored substance. They poisoned the waters and killed thousands of river dolphins outside of their pod, which was why his pod had to relocate and depart from their previous home. It was one of the last places that the humans had left alone.

The mystical structures covered in vines along with the dense forestation indeed portrayed the aura of a place untouched by modern civilization. Flooded ruins that had sunk below the mud provided protection from the sun and a safe food source of crustaceans who hid within the ground.

The sibling river dolphins had finally convinced their parents to let them go free today and it was a relief to be out in the world once more. But as the day sank down to dusk, it was better to be protected than to fall prey to the jaguars and snakes prowling in the dark.

Chapter 2

The jaguar prowled about the darkening jungle in search of prey that had lingered too long in the open. He stalked his targets from high in the trees looking down for a good, hearty meal. There it was, sauntering about the shadows of the evening: a tapir that had forgotten who ruled the jungle. He stealthily climbed down into a bush and approached, closer and closer, until he leaped. Claws sank into flesh and his quarry was dead before it could manage to make a sound, let alone fight for its life. The jaguar picked it up and hauled it into his hideout underneath a rocky outcropping behind a tangle of verdure.

As he savored his meal, the jaguar contemplated when his next hunt would be. He had recently heard more unusual sounds coming from the edges of the forest and was becoming warier of humans that had tried to trap him before. That time, he had barely gotten away with his life and realized that his power in the jungle only remained as long as he had no competition. He who had once been bold and daring, now rarely strayed from the den, afraid he would encounter human guns or other machines.

Curling up into a tight ball the jaguar prepared for sleep again, failing to notice soft sounds of leaves crunching beneath hiking boots in the distance as he shut out the world. The sound was coming from a couple who were touring the ruins nearby. Unlike others of their kind, they were no treasure hunters, but adventure seekers and avid field researchers that only wanted to explore for important data and desired a break from civilization.

"Put some mosquito repellent on, Lucille," coaxed the man, holding out a bottle in his firm but gentle hands. Most of his body was darkened like them, tanned from all of the time he had spent outdoors. His clothing was dark hunter green and, with his mocha-colored hair, he blended into the forest quite well. His wife, Lucille's lighter skin stood out, while her smooth dirty blonde hair fanned around her in the wind, making it appear like a halo around her head. She refused the mosquito repellent, insisting that its smell was too strong, and gripped a pair of binoculars tightly as if expecting something to happen at any moment.

Meanwhile, her husband held his phone and looked at it in desperation as a red dot bounced wildly around the screen.

"I can't get a signal!" he complained.

"Oh, don't worry about it, Justin. We're here to enjoy the jungle. Let's set up a tent in that cave. We can worry in the morning."

She held out her binoculars for one last glance around the dark jungle and backed into the cave. To her surprise, she found something behind her rather than in front as her ears picked up on a low growl. Resting in the darkness of the cave was a magnificent creature pawing and snarling at an invisible foe in his sleep. At first, the woman was startled, but after realizing that the creature was in a subconscious state, she called for her husband, Justin, to share such a moment with him, one that they would surely treasure for years to come. But they were careful not to take any photos or make any sound in fear of waking the animal from his slumber. Slowly, they backed out of the cave, parting ways with the majestic creature. They sought refuge in a clearing elsewhere while taking note of the jaguar's current location, should the need arise for that data.

Finding a small space amidst the jungle, Justin began hammering down stakes for their tent. On the other hand, Lucille took sight of an agouti in the vicinity, with mud coating its muzzle as it munched on small seeds.

Finally, Justin convinced her to lie down and it didn't take long for sleep to bring them into a night of peaceful oblivion.

Chapter 3

The young monkey got no rest that night, one of many sleepless nights to come. Her hunger was a more pressing issue than finding her troop, resulting in a draining search for food all day. She was no longer taking for granted the efforts of her dead mother, who had given her everything of her choosing without complaint. How she longed for those days back.

However, the young monkey would have to grow up and face the challenges that she would be up against.

Her thoughts soon became clouded with nostalgic memories of her deceased mother. Time could not be sped up and it was impossible for her to overcome the grief in such a short span of time. Finding a loophole in her vow, she reasoned that risking herself would not endanger others. This was how the young monkey became fascinated with the idea of revenge, picturing her hands ripping out human hair, her teeth tearing deep gashes into their skin, and other fanciful ideas much beyond her innocent age.

As for food, she had only managed to eat a few leaves before being chased away by another angry species of monkey that hissed and spit in alarm at the sight of her. She knew she would have to find a new troop soon. Too quickly, loneliness was catching up to her and she would have to hope for pity if she wanted another troop to take her in. At the very least, she could push herself to keep going if she received acceptance from others, if not the love she once cherished dearly.

Now she crawled on branches, still searching for fruit, unable to climb with aching arms. Noticing tufts of fur left behind on branches and small footprints in the mud, the young monkey made after her ex-troop thinking she could live off the scraps of their foraging. It would be obvious where they had stopped to eat, as their droppings would litter the ground, spreading seeds and preserving the forest for generations to come. She would do the same if only she could find food.

At some point, the endless motion of putting one hand in front of the other lulled the monkey into a trance-like state and she strayed off the path, heading into the unknown. She was fatigued, but kept going, eventually realizing she had no idea where she was. But to her left was the dulled yellow peak of a crane protruding into the sky and declaring its presence. That was her new destination. She would make the humans pay dearly.

But as she pushed herself to continue moving, the young monkey swayed on her feet and found herself falling, scraping her back on the branches. With the ground rushing up to her, she almost encountered death. However, fate was kind to her, and she was cushioned by an unusual material, smooth yet sturdy, that let her slide to the ground and become an easy target for predators big and small.

As her vision blurred, a human face appeared before her. She feebly clawed the human's arm, but the human picked her up and stroked her fur, cooing kindly.

"Look who I found, honey!" said the woman who had picked the monkey up. "It's only a little young monkey! Poor little thing. It must have gotten lost in the forest."

"What's that?" called a man, slamming the palm of his hand into his phone. "I still can't get a signal, Lucille."

"Oh, come here, you," the woman named Lucille said. "I told you before, Justin... relax."

She pushed the hand with the phone down and kissed him on the cheek. Then she held up the young monkey, now fast asleep.

"What is that?" asked Justin and poked it. "Is it dead?"

"No! Of course not. She fell from a tree and landed on our tent. We have to help her."

"Help her?" cried Justin. Then he saw his wife's withering glare. "I-I mean... Of course. Of course, we'll help her. I'm glad to...."

In a matter of seconds, the woman's demeanor changed dramatically, alternating between firm and nurturing.

"First, we'll need food; this monkey looks seriously malnourished, water, soft cloth, and use that phone of yours to figure out what monkeys use for sore muscles," she ordered and then massaged the monkey's back as she slept.

"Don't worry. You'll be fine, little girl."

The two fed the monkey after it woke and made it a makeshift covering that gave it shade from the hot sun that peeked through the gaps in the leaves. They found aromatic leaves and rubbed them on her back to prevent parasites and let her heal her muscles from their overexertion.

"What do you plan to do now?" asked Justin, skeptical. "Are you going to keep it as a pet?"

"Pet? No, no. We will keep it until we find it a troop or something of the sort," his wife answered, cringing at the word 'pet.' She put the young monkey back in her arms and talked to it once more with her soothing voice, "Aren't you just beautiful? Yes, you are... good girl."

She stroked the monkey's fur lovingly. It was as if the monkey could read the woman's affectionate thoughts, and relaxed in her hands, thoughts of vengeance forgotten.

Her husband, on the other hand, was still skeptical: "Do you know what imprinting is? We could end up killing the monkey if we go on like this. You know that, right?"

The woman ignored the truth in his words, instead mockingly asking the young monkey, "Isn't he a pessimist?"

Justin scowled at her words. He began to contemplate different scenarios in which he would not have to continue enduring this. Wringing the monkey's neck was one option, but then his wife would probably wring his. A more compromising mindset took over and he attempted to find a scenario in which all would be happy.

"See, we're not far from the city, honey. There ought to be a shelter there for this young one." he reasoned.

"Where it'll get put down in no more than two weeks!" she retorted harshly. "As if I would let that happen. Not all people care for animals."

If the monkey had heard this, she might have been more cautious. Unfortunately, the rocking of the woman's arms had put the small animal into a much-needed rest. Suddenly a cacophony of whooping and shrieking filled the treetops and droppings from the trees pelted the humans like hail.

"There's the family!" the man exclaimed, already relieved. "Throw the monkey up."

"Throw him up? Are you out of your mind?!" the woman accused. Thankfully, the troop was beginning to jump out of the trees and onto the ground with their long lanky legs, which made it easy for the woman to simply leave the monkey there, hoping the approaching troop would carry her off.

As the monkeys left, the woman thought of all of the happiness and joy saving just one animal had brought her.

"You know what?" she said. "I just did something good in the world. And I'm not done yet!"

"Honey..." the husband said, crestfallen at her naivety, but he didn't know quite how to continue.

Chapter 4

From his den, the jaguar heard the earsplitting shrieks of prey. A feast that, as best he could tell, from the distance of their calls, was easy, nearby food walking on the ground instead of up in the trees. Stretching his legs for breakfast, he slowly trotted out of his cave. However, the quiet sound of his paws on earth triggered the monkeys to disappear as quickly as they had come. Not even the sleeping young one, that the jaguar had eyed for his first kill, remained.

But now he noticed something new. Humans and their small encampment that he knew must be full of their murderous tools. With his keen senses, he could detect their lingering smells inside his cave, and he cursed himself for not being more vigilant. He knew that by this time today, it was lucky that he had even woken up alive.

The jaguar remembered the painful memories of the past, how he had been so foolish, and the strength he had somehow found to escape with his life. If only his mate did not have to pay the price.

It had been two years after he had left his mother. Two years where he had learned to fend for himself and truly rule the forest. He had established dominance over an older male and taken a vast territory for himself, where he taught animals the meaning of fear. But he was not cruel. He hunted fairly and only took as much as he needed, often taking pity on younger animals, and hunting elderly or sick, those who were to die soon anyway. Nevertheless, he had a presence to him that no other species could compete with.

It was a typical day: the Jaguar strutted around his territory patrolling and flashing his impressive pelt rather than staying hidden in shadows that dappled the understory. Although he did not plan to hunt, he instinctively picked up on every sound and was surprised when he heard something rustle behind him. The second he whirled around, he could hear footsteps on a branch above him, but when he looked up, a sleek body brushed against his and he saw, directly in front of him, the edge of a tail before it disappeared into green.

Thinking it was a newcomer who wanted to provoke him, the jaguar bounded in pursuit, disregarding strong odors that were coming to him. As he leaped into a clearing, he saw a jaguar in front of him, but it was not another male like he thought. It was a female.

She let out a low rumble and another male slinked out from behind a tree. He would have to win her love now.

The female backed off, leaving the two males with a clearing to fight. Snarling and pawing the ground, both circled each other, waiting for an opportunity.

The other jaguar struck first, slicing his paw through the air and the first leaped onto the newcomer, countering by putting all his body weight into his blow. He caught the other jaguar in the shoulder, who roared in pain, rearing back and pouncing. While he missed the original jaguar's head, he was able to drag his razor-sharp claws down the other's back and leave gashes that bled painfully.

Both jaguars panting for air, the exchange of blows went back and forth, but the original jaguar was severely injured and knew he would have to make his move soon. He ran straight toward his opposition and leaped over him, then pushed off a tree while in the air, and spun directly into the other jaguar, ripping his throat with his claws, and slamming his body into the forest floor. But, while his move had succeeded, he lay on the ground and was too weak to get up. The other jaguar snarled and paced around, preparing to strike, but was losing a lot of blood and gave up, leaving the first jaguar victorious.

He approached the female, who came out from the green leaves turned red and rested her neck upon his, accepting him as her mate.

They walked together as he showed off his territory to her and gave her fresh pudu as a meal. Both cats, deeply in love, did not know how much the humans had encroached upon their territory and ventured out to find a den. Too soon would they realize their mistake as they heard shouts coming from ahead.

Instead of climbing up in a tree or hiding, the couple advanced and met a group of humans holding sticks. In an attempt to ward them off, they growled and hissed and raised their haunches to appear larger, but the humans were not to be deterred. In fact, the expression on their faces seemed to be elation, which is the opposite of what one should feel when coming upon jaguars. Or so these jaguars thought.

Instead, one of the humans raised a stick and it made a loud crack, followed by the scent of fire.

Although the male stood his ground, the female collapsed in the mud, her once sublime coat now a sticky crimson mess. He ran to her frantically to do something, but her eyes were rolled back in her head; she was dead. Another man raised his stick and the jaguar bolted for the trees, climbing into a tall, dense mass of wood and leaves.

The man went back to his friends and they hauled the jaguar's mate away, leaving him helpless, afraid, and a changed animal.

Chapter 5

Sulking in a corner, the river dolphin munched absently on a crab, contemplating what his parents had said. The second he and his sister reached their pod, she complained about the fish he had eaten. His mother and father had lectured him about it but were genuinely confused about what he had against shrimp and lobsters that made him risk his life. The river dolphin did not tell them this, but he longed to swim free, explore, and glide along the forest floor during floods. Other members of his pod wouldn't understand. They had lived their lives, witnessed one death, and sunk into fearful submission to the humans.

And it was wrong.

However, the river dolphin was clever. He knew that if he said this, they would ignore the importance of his message and simply ask how could talk about death so casually.

Instead, he planned to leave soon, quickly and so unexpectedly that no one would notice for days, thinking he was swimming in nearby tributaries to explore. He would ask his sister once, even though he could guess her answer and already see her heartbroken face, and then disappear into the rainforest. Only to be seen if he chose to.

His sister floated before him, nudging him with her tail and asking if he wanted to play. Despite his mood, he had to say yes; she was always able to cheer him up. Whistling, she jumped out of the water and spiraled back in, slipping through a gap in the stone walls that sheltered them. He followed her, gazing at the eerie moonlight that turned tree branches into claws and the water into a silver blanket.

By using his sonar after diving underwater, the river dolphin searched for his sister and a midnight snack. He could stir up plenty of crustaceans with his snout, but he was in the mood for something more interesting. As he picked up on his sister, spinning in the water in front of him, he swam toward her and noticed something quickly approaching in the same direction.

The river dolphin swam closer to his sister to investigate until he realized the creature in the vicinity was an anaconda. Clicking rapidly, he alerted his sister and the rest of his pod to the danger, but wondered if his sister would be able to swim away from the long, sinuous apex predator that was closing in.

The snake's swirling green body was enchanting as it glided and twirled effortlessly through the water, but the river dolphin's sister hastened to catch up with the rest of the escaping pod.

Suddenly, cries filled the air adding to the already chaotic sounds from the river dolphins. A hunting party of indigenous Amazonians appeared from the trees and began their attack. It was a group of five men holding different sorts of tools that were being used in an attempt to bring the anaconda down. The snake's thick body was visible from the murky waters, but the river dolphins were hidden, the only sign of them being splashes in the water that could have come from any animal.

Three of the hunters wielded poison-tipped arrows, which they fired. Two penetrated the anaconda's flesh, but the other did not fly true, striking one of the many river dolphins and interfering with her sonar. Another man held up a blowgun, but the lethal dart he fired whistled harmlessly through the air and thunked into a tree. It was the final man who had the most power as he held a gun. It was of an old design, for that was all the native people could trade for, but it still contained much power within its metal body.

He had the anaconda's head in perfect range and was about to pull the trigger when one of his hunting partners cried out in surprise. The man had spotted the beached river dolphin that had been thrown off course by the arrow and ended up on the forest floor. Even though the people desperately wanted to save their tribe from the wrath of the anaconda, their shaman had taught them of the spirits' liking for the river dolphins and that it was bad luck to be part of one's death.

The men would not be like those whom they considered the brutes of modern civilization and treat other animals as if they were below their dignity, choosing to rescue the river dolphin. They rushed toward it as the rest of the pod escaped. Their insufficient attacks had been enough to take the snake's attention from the river dolphins, but they had only so much time to save this beached river dolphin. It could end up costing their lives.

One man worked on soothing the beached river dolphin, while the others slid a palm frond underneath its belly and eased it back into the river. It took off quickly and so did the tribal people, racing back to their homes and not at all regretting the fact that they had chosen to be better than those who had forcefully pushed them out of their homelands, by giving up an important hunt.

Chapter 6

The young monkey was alone once more. Immediately after she and the other troop of monkeys were out of the humans' eyesight, she was abandoned again. They had recognized her as a member of a rival troop. She didn't attempt to go after them; rather, she headed toward the crane, thinking that all of this drama had just been a big misunderstanding. If the humans who had just nurtured her back to health were so kind, the ones who killed her mother must have been as well. It was an accident, that was all. So she headed in that direction, not sure what she would do when she arrived, but persistent nevertheless.

She climbed and climbed just as she had before, but was now learning and could find more food. Not enough to sustain her growing body, but enough to keep her alive. She would be able to have more rest, too, as she could fit into small gaps between wood, sheltered from the night. Often that would result in hordes of insects crawling over her body when she woke, but she could differentiate the poisonous and edible ones well enough to eat most of them as revenge.

The monkey spotted a cluster of fruits higher up in the trees and scrambled toward it, unbeknownst of danger. She had barely put the first one in her mouth when a piercing scream came from behind her. It came from an eagle multiple times her size and he was clearly hungry too. But the monkey was not going to give her meal away so easily and snapped off the cluster of berries, proceeding to jump backward off the branch she was standing on. The eagle's silver beak snapped in anger and he dove with such speed that some of his snowy white feathers were left behind as he raced to grab the monkey from midair.

The monkey's maneuver was precarious, but it was a matter of life or death, in any case, and she did not want to feel the eagle's enormous talons snapping her neck. She had seen too many of her troop members being taken this way, the only warning sign being a slight shadow or single feather before powerful claws clamped down on a monkey; their sheer force and size were enough to kill almost any animal, even without the razor-sharp points.

As she reached the bottom of the canopy, her prehensile tail managed to latch onto a branch and shoot her skyward. All the eagle saw when he broke through the barrier of leaves was a stick plummeting downward, but it was not long before his facial feathers aroused him to the sound of the monkey scampering toward a tree hollow. The eagle flew upward, but a pair of arms pulled the young monkey into the wood just in time.

The young monkey looked around in panic and found curious, wizened eyes staring at her. It was another monkey of a different species and he was much older than her. They both looked at each other wonderingly, until their temporary sanctuary shook, and the eagle's beak protruded through the opening, snapping and cawing wildly. Without question, the two monkeys were a team and were fighting for their lives. But it seemed that the older monkey had experience with this and simply pushed the young monkey to the back of the hollow, unflinching at how close he had come to being shredded. The fearsome cries of the eagle continued as the two monkeys waited out the danger; eventually, he flew away, leaving the young monkey both unharmed and indebted. She tried to speak to the elder monkey, but her words were gibberish to him and it was the same when he tried to talk. It was actions that would allow them to communicate within their small world that only the light peeking through from the clouds could reach.

She offered him some berries, but beneath her energetic outlook, he could see how malnourished she was and declined. However, the young monkey did not want to be a burden and harm him in any way, like she was to her mother, so she began to leave the tree cavity. The elder monkey held her back, the look on his face making his meaning all too clear. They both knew she was not ready to survive on her own.

***

The jaguar shook his head to rid the last traces of the memory. The scars on his back that had never faded began to tingle as though they wanted to open again. To take his mind off the turn of events he had inevitably been part of, he headed to the river to swim and fish.

He walked along the riverbank for a while, dragging his tail in the water as a lure for unsuspecting fish and managing to catch a few by slapping them out of the water when he felt any sensation. Once he had eaten his fill, he paddled along the river and drifted quite far when he heard odd noises coming from ahead.

Knowing that it was probably plotting humans, he shook water droplets out of his body and approached, crouching low, blending in with the mixed darks and lights of the jungle, invisible.

The jaguar was correct. It was people creating the racket and disrupting various animals in their forest in a place some ways upstream from where the river became part of a canyon and then fell as a waterfall. He could not see them, but could hear that they were using their machines and probably building a fortress of some sort. He heard a good amount of humans and they were all conversing, but the jaguar had no idea what they were up to. All he believed was that it would be evil.

At the place itself, traces of oil and garbage were already running down the river from their work. And it would only get worse, for the plan was to finish a hydroelectric dam in that very spot, cutting off access to multiple tributaries that the river connected to. Once it was finished, it would affect the animals' ecosystem profoundly and cut off the food supply for many.

All the jaguar heard was the same species that had killed his mate. He was angry, and he was scared, and there wasn't a single thing he could do about it except run and hide.

But he didn't have much time to dwell on it, as the water rippled behind him and he turned to face a large caiman. Typically, their kind didn't bother his species as both were evenly matched, and only the element of surprise provided a substantial advantage. This time, he would be in for a fight. The caiman before him was giant, much bigger than he had ever seen them, meaning he would be more robust and well-shielded. Caimans' scaly bodies were hard to penetrate, while shock force did not affect them, but water and land worked in the jaguar's favor, while the caiman only dominated the water.

The caiman lashed his tail and the jaguar scratched the ground with his claws. This would indeed be a battle of the titans. And both competitors were ready to win.

Chapter 7

Buzzing filled the air, which was exactly what the couple was looking for. It was rhythmic and pulsating, made up of the wingbeats of dozens of entranced insects.

"I can hear it really well now. We're close!" exclaimed Justin.

"I still don't get why we're heading toward the enormous swarm of mosquitoes, but I have gotten to see a lot of lifers, so fair is fair, I guess," replied Lucille.

The Amazon Rainforest was the perfect destination for them, having multifarious flora and fauna, so each of them was able to fulfill their desires between seeing nature for enjoyment and collecting data for research, as well as enjoying a feeling of blissful isolation by being surrounded by wilderness. They had to be careful, too, making sure not to harm nature and leave behind damaging traces while ensuring that no harm would come to them in the form of a dangerous plant or animal. But this was second nature for the two conservationists who had spent their lives immersed in the same thrill they were now experiencing. Every step they took was a new adventure, with a complete feeling of peace and wonder after breathing in the fresh forest air. And the jungle inspired awe, as well, for marvels of nature were abundant here, even while humans continually threatened its very existence.

"There it is!" cried the man in excitement and he was beholden by a plant that was both beautiful and ugly at the same time. The species was a carnivorous flower, topped with innocent white petals, that had extended its tiny green branches outward. Vertical stalks and the clump-like spread made it clear to Justin that this was a sundew. However, it was extremely rare to be sighted in this area of the Amazon and only rumors had guided the search to find it.

While the husband was extremely intrigued, the wife was revolted and had taken to looking at a pair of toucans in their mating ritual. The male pestered the female, chasing her wherever she hopped, with treats, like fruit, and interesting objects that he liked to play with.

Meanwhile, the river dolphin had reached a spot in the river not so far away. In fact, he was quite close to these humans, but didn't know it yet. He had escaped from his pod after they had regrouped, following a brief conversation with his sister. She had been devastated, but was smarter than he gave her credit for and had already known his ideas for years before. So with everything settled, he had taken off into the unknown.

Now he was absorbing more new sights and sounds than he had in his entire lifetime, cowering beneath the ancient human ruins. Since his escape, he had discovered places beyond where his pod had ever ventured. At night, he used to dream of what lay beyond the zone where he was permitted to go. This was exactly what he had imagined, if not better. From observing different species of birds in the trees to the small rodents lapping at fresh water from the riverbank, but staying wary of predators that lurked, this was like a new world for him. Even some species of fish in the water were alien to his mind. And he could eat whatever he wanted when he was hungry, not just crabs all day.

The river dolphin kept swimming downstream and detected yet another new kind of fish with his sonar. This one was see-through and had an extremely small, circular face. The oddest part, though, was the fact that it had no fins or tail. And he really wanted to try it.

Although he did not attempt to be stealthy, the fish was still an easy catch and practically floated into the river dolphin's mouth. He bit down on it, expecting soft, sweet meat, but instead found himself being speared inside the mouth by a sharp material. The thing he had thought to be a fish was, in reality, a plastic bottle that had floated from a careless human into the Amazonian ecosystem, ending up within this river dolphin's mouth. The material was such that he could neither break it down to swallow nor force it out of his mouth, since it clung to his muscle tissue and shredded it with every breath he took. To make matters worse, his breathing rate had increased to no avail, as the plastic bottle prevented adequate air from reaching his lungs. The deprivation of oxygen further added to his state of panic, while he thrashed around in an attempt to dislodge the plastic from his soft inner tissue. Seemingly endless bleeding caused red liquid to flow into him instead of out, further increasing his inability to breathe. Eventually, he stopped flailing about and succumbed to the killer substance, letting the current float him away.

The couple, now just mere feet away, had yet to notice the river dolphin, as they were absorbed in the other biodiversity in the brackish water ecosystem. After searching out heliconias, bromeliads, and orchids following the sundew, the couple immersed themselves in the variety of creatures along the Amazon River's bank.

Both of them were crouched down and the husband got up only for a drink of water when he saw small red flowers blooming up from the water. Closer inspection brought the sight of the suffocating river dolphin to his eyes and although the experience with the monkey had been utter torture for him, he had to do something.

"Um," he began awkwardly, giving a nervous laugh, "Is- Is that a bottlenose dolphin I see there?"

“What’s that? There can’t be a bottlenose dolphin all the way out here. I mean the chances of–” she cut off after standing up, as well, and following her husband's horrified gaze. “Oh. So that’s what you meant. Well, stop standing around. Get me the scissors and tweezers from the first aid kit!”

The wife started slapping the water with her hand and playing recordings of river dolphin sounds on her phone. In his painful, disoriented state, the river dolphin thought he had found company and would not die alone, so the wife succeeded in luring him. Once the husband retrieved the required materials, he helped his wife cut and pick bits of plastic out of the river dolphin’s mouth, who soon could feel relief in his sore muscles that had been forced open for an unnaturally long time. However, he swiftly realized that there were no other river dolphins and attempted to escape, lashing out with his head and connecting with the husband’s shin.

The husband jumped in pain and dropped the tweezers he was holding. They landed on his wife’s hand, but she didn’t even flinch and mollified the river dolphin with long strokes across his head. She pried open his mouth without resistance and plucked the remaining plastic out, then let him float back into the river, tired and hurt, but alive to see another day.

Chapter 8

The young monkey was almost no longer quite young; she had seen her troop's behavior in the previous years and the new monkey in her life was just as helpful, preparing her for the future with knowledge that only experience could teach. She was nearing three years of age and the older monkey she was now living with knew that she would have to leave eventually.

At the moment, the young monkey was gorging herself upon passion fruit after she and the older monkey had followed other primates' traces to find a stash of the fruit. They had not been bothered since leaving refuge in the tree hollow, but the young monkey was warier of predators after the experience with the eagle. Going back to the crane was no longer her goal, for she had become more sensible with company, but it was still a passing thought in her mind and nagged her when she longed for peace.

After eating her fill, the young monkey jumped around and cuddled with the older monkey, who was unused to affection since being alone for so long. He returned a caring hug and watched as the young monkey stretched her arms in weariness.

As the skies darkened, the two returned to their cozy dwelling and slept, thankful for the companionship that filled the once-empty spaces in their hearts with love.

Crepuscular rays were further filtered through gaps between leaves in the treetops as the sun arose, the canopy acting like window blinds for the animals still awakening. As she opened her eyes, the young monkey felt the older monkey grooming her and picking debris out of her fur. The simple action filled the small monkey with emotion as it showed true acceptance and reminded her of her mother doing the same to her almost every day. Thus far, she had been holding back the memories of her mother to hold back the pain, but now that the dam was broken, the water would not stop flowing. Vivid images flashed through the young monkey's mind and she felt so much guilt. If only she had listened and not gone on to explore the crane.

She did not once consider the fact that it was the humans' fault because the crane driver had created such a traumatic experience that she could scarcely remember the reality of the incident. He had damaged the very core of her cognitive abilities and had scarred her mentally for life. That, paired with the kindness from other humans previously, incurred a mix of fear, sadness, and culpability. Her thoughts now turned to the older monkey. She would never be able to repay him for his generosity and the least she could do was keep him safe. Hence, she made the decision to leave instantly, not wanting another death on her hands and thinking that all she would do was put him in danger, somehow, in some way.

Before she could be stopped, she was up and out of the cavity in the tree and had disappeared before the older monkey could catch up. The young monkey was returning to her mother's body to forever mourn her spirit, something nothing could touch, not even death.

Brachiating with adrenaline-powered speed, she was able to reach close to the crane unscathed, physically at least. From here, she hoped to be able to locate her mother and wished that the monkeys who used to be her troop did not come back to mourn as well.

***

The battle had already begun, but came to an impasse quickly. The jaguar was too quick on his feet, but the caiman had too much brute force for the nimble cat to overcome. As night approached, the caiman had sunk below the water, neither prolonging the fight nor giving up, and the jaguar had waited by the riverbank, leery.

Day arose, but neither animal wanted to make the first move, so they waited each other out, making small bluffs to trick the opponent into attacking. The caiman suddenly lunged forward and nearly latched onto the jaguar's leg. However, he was quick to dance around the sharp teeth and retaliated by cuffing the caiman in the eye, temporarily blinding him with the mud he left behind. Although the jaguar's claws were not retracted, his strike did not penetrate the caiman's tough skin and only the inside of the paw made contact.

He got in a few more hits by launching his body into his attacks, rotating three-fourths of the way around to cover more range before that caiman entered his element in the water. However, the jaguar was just as good a swimmer and unhesitatingly leaped into the river, pushing the caiman under the water. The caiman retaliated by thwacking his tail into the jaguar's leg, making him lose his advantage for a moment so the caiman could escape. But it was futile, as the jaguar easily flipped his opponent over and bit the caiman right where his head met his body. He thrashed once, twice, and then he was dead, as simple as that, and the jaguar swam it to shore, bearing the tremendous weight of the creature that was longer than himself.

Reaching shore, the jaguar dragged his kill into a dense thicket and tore into the belly, staining his teeth and muzzle red. The caiman's mouth was splayed open while the jaguar ate his meal, as if he were to come alive at any second, snapping and attacking, but the jaguar had been quick to get its kill spot without sustaining any injury.

However, in the attack, the jaguar had forgotten about the humans and their project, which was going to be a hydroelectric dam in the Amazon. Luckily, no one saw him and the caiman fight, and he could feast in peace for now, but using a hydroelectric dam could severely impact him and other animals even more than direct confrontation.

Following his hearty meal, the jaguar draped himself across a shaded branch to nap, making up for lost sleep from the previous night. While drifting off, the already humid air of the Amazon Rainforest became palpably thick as large clouds rolled in and released sheets of rain. Droplets were caught by leaves and flower petals that bent down as if to release water into the ground, but sprung back up, until water gathered at their edges and fell in a steady rhythmic beat. Various hues within the forest now became glossy as surfaces that were colored covered themselves in streaks of rain. The tree that the jaguar had chosen to rest in was dense enough and he opted to continue sleeping.

Even more moisture was added to the mix as warm air blew in from the distant ocean. Still, the warmth did not bother any of the forest animals because of the cloud cover that sheltered the Amazon's life from the full intensity of the equatorial sun. Ever lingering mist that hung at the peaks of tall trees was now all the more pronounced, showing, clearly, why these parts of South America were called the "cloud forests."

Reptiles and birds flourished in the wetness. Frogs crawled out from their hiding places and filled the forest with croaking. The variety of colors on them made the brown trees look like they were covered in colored splotches and brushstrokes of paint. Shining hummingbirds stopped darting around from place to place and came to rest on branches so thin that the wind could break them. Macaws flocked together in their family groups and fluttered their wings, making splashes in the water. Many preened themselves and fluffed out their feathers, a true sign of comfort and relaxation.

The pristine calmness and mirror-like reflection of the river were shattered as water droplets bore holes into its surface. Throughout the Amazon, the snaking body of water flooded parts of the forest floor, sweeping dead and fallen leaves in, along with the insects that called them home, making perfect food for the multitudes of residing fish.

The jaguar flicked his tail to combat flies attracted to his moist fur. He stretched his paws and neck, then flopped back onto the moistening branch. But the water did not bother him. In fact, it was one of his many joys in the rainforest.

Chapter 9

Swerving from side to side, the river dolphin swam swiftly through the flooded river, anxious to return to his pod. He could already see their reactions, but he was willing to sacrifice that much to stay hidden from the dangers of the outside world. He was never going back after his mishap with the plastic bottle, however enticing the other fish seemed.

While the forest floors were submerged and could provide easy shortcuts to get the river dolphin to his desired location, he was too afraid to diverge from the paths he had come to know well, relying heavily on muscle memory to get through the murky water that had risen in height due to the rain.

At this point, he could not be sure whether he would even be able to find his family as they could have relocated after the incident with the anaconda, but hope was the only thing he had. Hope and fear. Both feelings drove him faster and he reached the ruins quickly, but no one was in sight, so he pushed on, against the raging current.

Eventually, the rain let up and his swimming in the water became normal like before. He cut through it effortlessly, making only the slightest ripples and showing no sign of resistance from the current, like he was part of the water itself. But what he wanted was to be part of his pod again, which was why he exerted his muscles to their maximum capacity as he swam on and called desperately for someone, anyone, to hear.

Without realizing it, the river dolphin swam into a separate tributary, flowing away from the central Amazon River and heading in a different direction than he truly wanted. And although he didn't know it, he was also approaching the sounds of the hydroelectric dam project that the jaguar had heard before.

The group building the dam consisted of many people and they were in the finishing stages of their project. Since the dam itself was completed and only a few more things were needed to make it operational, it seemed it would be soon when the full project would truly be completed. For now, the group relaxed beneath their tents, taking in the smell of the plants after rainfall as the water level of the flooded river receded and the tropical paradise of the Amazon let the sun shine above the brush and emergent layer of trees.

***

The young monkey, who was practically mature now, had waited out the rain in the trees and after the flooding swept away mud and leaves, it was easy to locate her mother's body. Time had taken the appearance of life from the dead monkey, leaving a mangled heap of bones and muscle rotting while being eaten by flies and other parasites. The young monkey cradled what appeared to have once been the head and screamed at the sky, full of emotion. She then put her hand in her mother's and groomed what was left of her fur: disheveled chunks cast among a pattern of dried mud and shriveled muscle tissue.

She ended up deciding that if this was where her mother died, it would be her resting place as well. Now, she went to gather acai berries and ate all but one, which she placed in her mother's palm and closed her fingers around it.

Suddenly, a growl from the nearby crane snapped the monkey out of the melancholic peace she was experiencing.

Wondering how such a massive creature could move with such speed and ease, the monkey climbed up into the sky, breaking through a dense cover of branches and leaves to view the scene. She was struck by a sight unlike any other in her lifetime. Small fires burned throughout an empty, barren wasteland of orange soil. More monsters like the humans' crane rumbled, carrying fallen trees. Bats' and birds' bodies littered the scene, dead amongst the edges of the forest. And humans were everywhere, shouting and piloting the evil metal beasts that could fell trees with such ease. Already, so much of the forest was gone; what once stretched for miles as a sea of green was now simply nothing.

The barren remnants of the once-lush forest were filled with humans and their contraptions, but the monkey remembered the humans who had been so kind to her. She thought that all she needed was the correct approach to make the humans see reason. After all, no animal could be as greedy and truly destructive as them. Out of hopefulness and curiosity, she cautiously approached the camp, praying that the death of these rodents, reptiles, other animals, and, unforgettably, her mother were simply accidents by these gentle beings. But before she could get any closer, the tree she was perched on gave way and she was barely able to leap to another for safety, hiding in its growth.

"Yeah, that's it!" one human said, slapping the man operating the tree cutter, with vicious teeth all around its rotating body, on the back. "At this rate, we'll be knocking down the forest in days.

"Daw's getting the hang of it!" another said in a playfully teasing tone. "He's not that much of a newcomer anymore. Soon enough, he'll have more timber than me!"

More men came to transfer the logs onto trucks to haul them away and make profit in civilization, selling all kinds of items without people knowing the sustainability of what they were buying. The corpse of a parakeet that had fallen from the recently cut tree was unnoticed by the humans and squelched under the heel of one of their boots. The oaf who had done it looked down momentarily and simply squished it a bit more before he continued walking.

"Whatcha got on your feet there, Gary?" one asked, observing the maroon mess upon the person's leather boots.

"Yuck!" the man with the boots replied in dismay. But his face showed otherwise. He seemed gleeful and triumphant as could be. Another innocent squirrel's body was trampled underfoot by the man, this time taken no notice of. It was just one of the many such happenings between all of the people working at the site.

The monkey, unfortunate enough to have observed the gruesome death of some of its fellow jungle dwellers, kept putting off the idea that any of this had been intentional. But her sense of reason sent her fleeing back to her mother's body so she would have to see no more. The hope that such accidents were plentiful in a dedicated project like the humans' was present in her mind, even though it was entirely against her logical thinking. She was fighting an internal conflict with herself as she knelt beside her mother's corpse and something in the back of her mind, despite her conscious self thinking otherwise, realized that she was lucky her mother's body was not disgracefully squished below the heel of a boot as well.

Chapter 10

Awaking from his short siesta during the rainfall, the jaguar sharpened his claws against tree bark and chewed on a twig. He climbed down from his resting place and batted around a mouse before pinning its tail to the ground and then letting it run away with fear instilled deep into its tiny heart. This suffering was what the humans made the jaguar experience and he felt the need to establish dominance in some way, but it was not often that he resorted to diverting his mind in a sadistic manner. He had remembered the humans by the river again and was even more fearful. Twice humans had recently invaded his territory and twice had he failed to notice them when he needed to. His peaceful trance from sleep had been quickly broken as the memories came, but there was nothing he could do now except cower in his den, until that was invaded again, as the humans had earlier.

He trotted through leaves and mud, taking in deep whiffs of air to ensure nothing had come near as he had slept. Once, being a young and mighty male jaguar had been so easy and empowering, but now it seemed like it only brought on a life of constant worry.

To gain back the sense of relaxation he had gotten from his reposeful nap, the jaguar dove into the river and paddled along its breadth. He put his head underwater for some moments and released a breath, causing bubbles to distort and pop at the surface. Rising from below the water, he gulped in air, purred at the cool, calming feeling the river brought him, and decided to patrol his territory. The river was a natural boundary of it, so he walked alongside the water, frequently clawing trees and urinating where it was necessary. In total perimeter, his land was large, so he sped up the process by cutting through the forest and only marking in occasional places where he needed to. The jaguar was confident enough that his might could ward off a young male should the need arise.

The process took many hours and brought him into the evening. He proceeded to stalk a deer from afar to spare himself the effort of a chase. When the deer knelt to eat a few blades of grass, the jaguar got close enough to crouch, preparing to pounce. It was a perfect ambush; the jaguar killed his prey before the deer knew what was happening with a quick snap of the neck. The name "jaguar" truly suited this formidable animal, characterizing his ability to kill with one leap.

After eating, he grew tired of the day and lay on his side upon a rock with his front legs bent slightly and back legs extended. As his mind drifted off, the muscles in his face relaxed, letting his ears droop down on his head. The jaguar's breathing became shallow and his belly rose and fell to the ground beneath him, hard and strong in actuality, but comforting for its presence against his skin in the night.

***

Clicking and whistling for hours on end had brought the river dolphin no closer to finding his pod. It seemed that isolation was now his fate, whether he liked it or not. After all, he had chosen to leave, and in doing so, left behind so much more than just a pod.

Night had come and the only thing to do was to stir up food from the mud and silt of the river to eat, as more efforts to call his family would likely be put to waste. He would rest for now, although sleep was surely a long way coming, but, by the morning, he would keep going down the river, even against its rapids if he needed to.

Floating on his side, the river dolphin left his upper eye open and shut down the opposite side's brain. He alternated through the night to keep watch for predators while getting enough rest, but no other animal bothered him. It was internal torment that he had to face.

Daybreak came slowly with a dawn chorus of birds that sang rich melodies to wake the forest. The river dolphin's sleep had not been restful, acting merely as a recharge to keep searching because it was the only thing he could do now.

Up ahead, the river became the bottom of a canyon that formed intense rapids, with creamy foam slamming rocks against each other, disintegrating them into a fine steam-like powder that wafted through the air. The river dolphin did not have great vision, as he relied on his sonar for hunting, so it would be dangerous to get through. But if this attempt would cost him his life, so be it. All he wanted now was to see his family, no matter the cost he would pay in the process.

Something snapped and tumbled down from above, falling into the abyss of churning water, never to be seen again. Once more, the river dolphin only had hope, and he was willing to follow it. Although that had not helped at all so far. Astray among jagged rocks along the sides of him were the remains of daring creatures who had ventured to do the same thing this river dolphin was about to do.

The river dolphin attacked, driving his body forward like a lance and diving into the flurry of it all. He was thrown around in every direction but managed, at the last second, to twist his body so it glanced off a wall and was forced back into the pummeling tides. Rocks pelted his smooth skin, creating nicks and scratches of various intensities. The pain was only enhanced by the brackish water that filtered salt into his wounds.

In this new part of the river dolphin's treasured river, it seemed death was the only possible outcome.

And then, from the swirling black and blue dots that flashed before the river dolphin's eyes, came calm, so sudden and unexpected that the river dolphin kept spinning himself forward long after being free. As he looked up at the welcoming blue sky, the canyon disappeared behind him, already forgotten. In front of him was the Amazon as he had never seen it before: an aerial view that encompassed the continuation of the long winding river he was on and all of the forestland that remained from the humans. It was a truly humbling sight and astonishing, as well. Until the river dolphin realized that he was about to dive headfirst down a waterfall.

The river dolphin pitied himself for having to sacrifice being engulfed by a gorgeous view of the rainforest so that his survival instincts could attempt to salvage this nearly lost cause. He paddled backward with his tail, but the current was too strong and all he managed to do was spin in circles. Before long, the river dolphin's frantic movements translated into his flailing in midair as he landed, but the water crashing into the ground cushioned the river dolphin's frenzied fall and he was able to right his body before the current swept him away again.

Behind him, the true grandeur of the waterfall was revealed as crystals spun through the air and struck the ground, bursting into thousands of shards: stray droplets amid a thundering cascade of water. Through a narrow strip of land that separated this tributary from the mainstream Amazon River, he observed some of the fish that dwelled upon the mysterious waters of the river. One pierced through the water, just as the river dolphin longed to do, and for a split second, this sight reignited the hope that his pod was within his reach. However, this large, scaly fish jumped not for the pleasure that he and his pod did, but to snatch a lizard basking in the warm sun of the tropical rainforest.

The lizard was quick to escape, darting across the water on flipper-like feet, but the fast fish was able to catch up and ensnare the prey in terrifyingly sharp teeth that lined its mouth and tongue. By river dolphin's estimations, this fish outsized himself and even some of the bigger members of his pod. The fish slowly retreated into the murky waters that were its refuge with a loud gulp that emanated in the water, a warning for all other prey to avoid meeting the same fate as the lizard.

Chapter 11

The meager fruit supply that the humans had left the monkey with was not enough to satisfy her appetite and she went to search for fruit and leaves. She instinctively followed her nose and climbed toward the enticing scent, locating a cluster of figs not too far away. To her dismay, the pile of figs that lay in the open was claimed by other animals. Two toucans, who were enjoying this meal immensely, guarded them under their wings. Flanking the other side of the bird was a fleeing rodent, hungry enough to attempt thievery of the figs and being frightened away by loud threats.

The monkey took her chances elsewhere, scouting out a tree that would provide her with bark and leaves. She picked off the outer edging of the wood, where decay had left its mark, and chewed the plant material thoroughly. From another tree came both the scent and sound of crunching, luring the monkey toward it. The monkey, following the noise, peeled away more rotting wood to find insect larvae that were easily captured by her hands. They had been boring into the tree, giving it a slow and painful death as most invasive species did. Although the monkey did not know it, these particular baby insects' parents were brought here by the humans and were slowly destroying the forest, bit by bit.

Soon, she climbed her way back to her mother's body, staying away from the humans nearby for now, since she had yet to formulate a plan.

To the monkey's horror or elation, she did not know, but another monkey was craning his neck to look at the remains of her deceased mother. When he heard her approaching, he turned his head to look at her and was instantly smitten. A friendly look crossed his face after their eyes made contact, as if to say, "'I knew I'd find someone!" He had a striking resemblance to the old, wise monkey that had taken this monkey under his arm for protection. However, he was much younger and the same kind of monkey as herself. The unique fur of this other monkey that had bamboozled the monkey into thinking he was of another species, once again, caught her eye. It was a more kapok brown shade than she was used to. They approached and acknowledged each other in harmony.

They observed each other's coats, stroking the tails of the other. From growling and additional vocalizations they emitted, the monkey learned that this male was of another troop where everyone donned this unique pelt. The monkey told her new friend that she was lost from her troop. He immediately confided that he had been recently separated from his own.

She sat upon his lap as acceptance and the two became mates that very day, once the male accepted in return, wrapping his legs and arms around her. However, she kept the condition that they would stay by her mother to honor and mourn her life and death, despite the fact that any member of their species would struggle to flourish in an edge habitat near loggers.

The newcomer, now her mate, had wanted to take her to his family so she could join his troop, but they were nowhere to be found in the forest. Exploring too far away from the monkeys he had grown up with, the male was unable to locate them.

***

Long after morning had come, the jaguar awoke from his long sleep and basked in the sun for warmth, but didn't feel like doing much else.

Heat from the forest entered his fur and was trapped by the shining golden coat that attracted light to its flowery rosettes. He rested his head in between the gap of one branch separating into two, gazing down at the ground below him. The warmth on his skin made his mind fuzzy and dulled his senses, but it was worth it for the relaxation it brought him. At any rate, this would keep him satisfied for the day, but he planned to scan the edges of his territory for any more human activity. They had already surrounded him and were slowly closing in, so he had an inclination for keeping track of when he would have to escape the place he had worked so hard to earn and protect.

As a cloud drifted between the sky and his resting, the jaguar leaped to the ground and left the river, toward where he knew a group of humans resided. He would be highly cautious there and, afterward, planned to head toward a place where their machines towered above the forest, for human activity had grown increasingly. With a steady pace, the jaguar was able to reach his first destination quickly enough and observed from darkness, turning invisible in the shadows. He was only a pair of eyes, blinking from the undergrowth, unnoticed by any.

The place was a tourist residence for people who came to visit the rainforest and wanted to be immersed in it. Outside, children ran around and chased each other, creating such high-pitched noises that the jaguar struggled not to put his head on the ground and attempt to cover his ears. Parents had more serious expressions than their carefree kids as they negotiated with the tour guide, but had to smile at the kids' delight. The accommodations themselves were warm and welcoming, but, at the same time, it seemed like an unassuming, run-down log cabin, possibly to provide the residents with a greater sense of being enveloped in wilderness. Patrolling among the edges of the area were somber-faced guards with modified pistols to protect the people from wildlife.

As if the wildlife didn't need protection from them.

Meanwhile, the jaguar seemed relieved that the motives of the people here were not anything more than personal enjoyment and headed toward his next stop. In fact, the playful laughter of the gleeful children conjured nostalgic memories of the jaguar play fighting with his sibling. But that was all in another time and another life, best forgotten now.

A troop of monkeys shrieked and scattered as the jaguar walked into a clearing beside the spot where he was suspicious of human activity. His destination was the very same deforestation site that the monkey was so ignorant of. Seeing such horrendous sights like toxic smoke destroying vital cloud cover and shredded trees coming out from a wood chipper ensured, for the jaguar, that his worries were veracious.

Without noticing his movements, he had stridden forward when a tree had been cut beside him. It fell slowly, however, the act of darting beneath it to safety revealed the presence of the jaguar to all of the loggers.

Chapter 12

"Dr. Jacobson, I think we're ready to test the valves and floodgates," offered a woman clad in navy blue clothing with a construction hat and orange vest.

"Alright Jessica, but make sure that all the systems are ready to go and check that everyone will be safe. Great work so far!" replied a slightly harassed-looking woman. She wore a black suit and gray pants, clearly the head of this operation, which was the building of a hydroelectric dam. Scribbling on a clipboard and tucking an auburn curl behind her ear, she looked up at the workers and smiled despite how weary she felt. She knew this project would turn out great. At first, the process had been painstakingly slow, but now they were almost ready.

"Ok, release the last floodgate now, we'll see if it's going to flood. So, three, two, one, now!" ordered Jessica to the people operating the controls.

The gush of water only temporarily unsettled the water level, but it quickly returned to normal when they closed the floodgate. As the increased thrumming of the Amazon River had not resulted in a flood when the floodgate was open, it was concluded by the team that the dam was mostly operational. They just had to do more tests and needed to monitor it closely.

"That's all for now. Prepare the turbines for later so we can check the electricity production. And great job, everyone, for your work," said

Jessica and headed to Dr. Jacobson to discourse over the successful results of their trial run.

***

Lucille and Justin were planning to head back to the city from which they had arrived in the rainforest, but kept getting sidetracked by all they had yet to see. They each would drag the other by the arm to go see some unique species and stop each other to inspect every part of the diverse landscape. Eventually, the two decided they could extend their stay. It was for research, after all.

They hadn't yet been deep within many of the rainforest's microhabitats, and one sure to be a highlight of their adventure was the gems hidden within the Amazon River. In their planning for the trip, both discovered a nearby place from where they could rent kayaks and walk them to the river. Putting off the excursion until the end of their journey because it was quite a long walk with the kayak to the river, they had decided only to do it if they felt up to the challenge.

Now seemed like the perfect moment. They hiked toward the location and were closer to it than they had thought. The place had been recommended to the couple through an online guide, so they didn't know much about it, but it seemed welcoming enough.

The two were immediately greeted by an enthusiastic tour guide who began a rant about the 'deal of a lifetime' and 'great quality with cheap prices,' but he was easily tuned out by Lucille and Justin, who had met enough profiteers in their travels to decide how much of swindling they were willing to tolerate.

As they paid for the kayak and left their IDs as collateral, Justin thought he heard something in the jungle and asked Lucille to listen. But she could not hear anything, so he thought nothing of it as the two each held one end of the faded tangerine-colored kayak above their heads, the paddles resting on top, and hiked toward the river.

Chapter 13

The jaguar had been running as fast as his strong legs could take him, away from the humans, away from the place that had an omen of death, not looking back to see what terrible things could be chasing him. He leaped over logs, rocks, and even other animals, quickly escaping from the horror into the forest. The second he stopped to rest, he heard human footsteps behind him and was forced to run again. But as fast as he had escaped one clearing, he was into another. The tour residences came into view before him and his momentum drove him into the side of one of the cabins. He was panting for air as the children screamed and ran. Whereas they were still full of energy, his exhaustion seemed endless. The adults frantically ran to the guards, too eager to hide behind a gun.

He rose to his paws just as the first bullet struck him. The powerful piece of lead meant to hit his head slammed through his shoulder, separating his leg from the rest of his body except for strong sinews that managed to hold together. But his bones were crushed, and red flowed everywhere, coming outside of him and going back into him as well. The nerves in his leg gave out and it collapsed beneath him, exposing his neck to the sky as a predator should never do.

When the second bullet whizzed through the air, he flopped to the ground with the reflexes that only an experienced big cat can have, but although it missed his neck, the small killer dragged along his flank, penetrating deep. Below the ripped skin and shredded muscle were punctured organs that sprayed blood and other puke-colored fluids in all directions, along with shattered bones that once held up the magnificent body of the jaguar.

The pain was too much, even as the jaguar only suffered a fraction of the pain because of all his damaged nerve endings. He wanted it to end, he wanted his suffering to be gone, he wanted his beautiful pelt to be free of its rust-colored stains, and the final bullet ended it all. It hit him right between the eyes, destroying his skull and ripping a hole straight through his brain. Even those who had done the killing looked sick and parents averted their eyes while covering their childrens', who wanted to look since they did not understand what had happened.

The miasma of death was everywhere as the short, plump tour guide in a safari-style jacket frantically apologized to all the families, while constantly reminding them of the small print in the insurance policy and the no refunds offered.

"I'll tell you about fine print!" a man bellowed after seeing the destroyed body of the jaguar, "In fact," he said, chuckling in a manner that was both sarcastic and angry, "The print wasn't even that small! It said right there, in the title, 'Amazonian Wildlife Tour.' This jaguar is Amazonian wildlife, correct? What should have been a memorable part of our tour has turned into a sickening experience for everyone! I don't care that it's dead, but in that manner?"

He spat on the ground.

"Well, well, well," said a gruff voice, leaving no room for the flustered tour guide to offer any reply, "Looks like we've got ourselves a dead jaguar!"

"And you are?" the guide asked, further bamboozled.

"Daw 'Sawdust' Miller. I am a part of a team that strives to bring the best quality products to your homes from right here in this pristine jungle. We also have authority to seize shot animals from around here and bring them back to the city for proper...," he trailed off, contemplating his next words, "disposal."

"Take it away? Are you mad? Do you know the price this thing can fetch?" piped up an eager woman from the tourists.

"Of course, I do," thought Daw, but instead said, "Well, we wouldn't want to be breaking the law now, would we? That would be like the company I work for logging without legal permits." Daw instantly regretted the words, and instead tried to cover up by adding, "And anyway, whoever performed the shooting did an awfully terrible job. I know a guy named Bruce who could... Never mind. The point is, it's worthless. You've broken the bones, stained the pelt, destroyed the skull. So, it's mine."

"Is not!" cried the tour guide indignantly, trying to salvage what was left of the tourists' interest by sticking up for the women who had spoken.

"No one," Daw said warningly, with much bravado, "Messes with Sawdust. And don't bother following me." He smirked, starting to drag the corpse beside him to wherever his encampment lay.

"Now you hold on just a second!" shrieked the tour guide, snatching the gun from his guard. However, his muscle-deprived body could barely keep up its weight, so it wasn't a very intimidating threat when he said, "Put your hands in the air!"

"Well, I can tell by the modifications of your *prized* piece, it holds a maximum of three bullets. And by the looks of it, we have exactly...," Daw paused to mockingly count the areas of puncture on the jaguar's body with his fingers, "Three shots. Your gun isn't loaded," he said, tsking with glee in his eyes, and pulled out his own revolver, "Lucky for me, mine is,"

The man named Daw disappeared into the shadows, hauling the ruined jaguar corpse along with him. The children cowered in fear behind their parents, who shielded them from the conflict.

"Serves you right not to make any profit!" yelled the man who was protesting about the fine print, "At least he's doing what he's paid for!"

Chapter 14

Although it was the same rainforest, the river dolphin felt like he had entered a new world. There was so much beauty in life here, for death could come at any second. But it was never long and dragged out, always quick, within fractions of a second.

After the lizard and gargantuan-sized fish, he had watched a hummingbird flit about, but as it neared a flower, a yellow vine morphed into a viper and swallowed the bird whole. Then a frog rested on the riverbank as a rat ate it alive and then keeled over, dead as well, because of the frog's poisonous glands and skin. In the trees, a sloth lazily inched upward, munching on its leaves upon ascent, but freezing as an eagle called hungrily.

Adding to the wonder this new world inspired, the river dolphin spotted what was another ancient temple. It was quite like the one he had lived by before, consumed by vines and trees that dominated the background of this scene. The dolphin yearned to explore it, but it brought back the pain of remembrance of his pod. And it was too far out to risk, as the growth of water plants was too dense, clouding his sonar.

As he kept swimming further, he thought he saw the familiar bump of a dorsal ridge and heard clicks coming from the water, but it couldn't be his pod. He was sure of that much by now. However, his curiosity was piqued, and he went toward what he thought he had seen.

To his surprise, a different kind of river dolphin inhabited the waters before him. The only way he could tell the contrast was because of the other river dolphins' longer bodies and slight differences in structure. It was a shock, nevertheless, for he had not ever thought beyond his home territory about different species before now, much less another kind of river dolphin. They attempted to communicate and found that they understood each other, despite their physical differences in appearance.

Relieved to have company, the river dolphin's pangs of loneliness vanished, even though this would only be for a short while. The other pod was not going to take him in, but advised him to be wary of the humans ahead and recommended that he stay off the main Amazon River to avoid caimans that lurked.

As he left them behind in the evening light, they offered another word of advice that he found quite odd. They told him never to approach anything new and to stay away from everything that he could. It seemed that they had submitted to fear, just like his pod.

***

While they were both separated from their families now, the monkey and her mate were enjoying life after finding a banana tree and eating lots of the fruit. They had then climbed up into higher trees and began to groom each other right as rain started falling. Their evening perch kept them dry and the humidity was blocked out by their fur that trapped warmth for the night. The tall, isolated tree they had chosen to retire in gave them peace of mind from predators and the male, having listened to the monkey's retelling of the experience with the eagle, was understanding and agreeable. Soon, two mates' eyelids grew heavy, and, snuggled close together, they slept in tranquility, comforted by each other's presence.

After a good rest, the two monkeys yawned, stretched their arms, and took to the trees, swinging in synchronization. With a mischievous glance at each other, they veered off to the side and plopped down in front of a nest, while a parent was off to find food. They found the reaction on three baby chicks' faces hilarious and mildly terrorized some other helpless baby birds before climbing after each other around trees that gradually got higher and higher in the sky.

Peeking their heads out from behind a thin branch high up, the two monkeys were so high that they could almost touch the low-hanging clouds. Scanning the horizon, their cute beady eyes saw far and wide, but the male was astonished by the emptiness where the loggers had left their mark. He realized how close the border of the devastation was to his mate's mother and turned to her, prepared to interrogate away. But before he could make a sound, she told him about the kind humans and the crane and her mother.

The wails escaped her mouth before she could stop them. Although it had been weeks ago, the pain was still fresh, and she relied on her mate for support. But he pushed her away as if revolted and took off into the jungle.

Even more grief filled her heavy heart as she clambered over branches after him. She couldn't lose him too. Not like her mother, not like the older monkey who had helped her. She rushed after him and easily caught up, seeing something that added even more guilt to her mind. Her mate was loyal until the end, dragging her mother's remains away from the loggers. He had not given up on her, but proven his love in a way she never knew he could.

She jumped onto the ground and rushed to him, intertwining his tail with hers. She may have still made amends for her faithlessness until the first tree crashed through the sky, landing mere inches away from where they were.

***

A group of men sat on small folding chairs in a circle beneath a large canopy tent. Out in the open lay the dead jaguar that Daw had stolen so cleverly from the tourists. It was the topic between the men right now as men congratulated Daw for his catch.

"So, how'd ya do it?" one of them asked.

"Oh, it was easy. Took it right off the ground and they didn't suspect a thing. I expect Bruce here can tell us a thing or two about what to do with it," replied Daw, basking in his glory and milking it for all it was worth.

"Say, Bruce," began another man, "why did you give up your profession and come to become one of us at your peak?"

The man that appeared to be Bruce simply answered that he had thought it was time to do something less unlawful, but the man was clearly reminiscing his glory days and chose to share one particular time that stood out to him.

"I remember I was hunting one of those pandas out in China and I reckon I did a better job of killing it than the rotten work done to the jaguar. Sliced its head right off and disemboweled it, in two clean strokes. Just the right amount of gore for me, while keeping the pelt and meat intact."

This, visibly, was impressive to the people, including Daw, but he brought the topic of the conversation back to himself, wanting more praise. Addressing one of his co-workers out in the field, or rather the forest, he shouted for the other to go easy on tree-cutting because the jaguar pelt would fetch enough money as it was. This choice of words brought him the desired result and babble broke out amongst those he was sitting with.

"How much do you think it's really worth, Daw?" whispered a younger voice, awe-struck by his daring to speak in the presence of a seemingly revered man. He was not very old, likely a high-school dropout that had found his way into this illegal business corporation.

"Over a hundred easy for the fangs alone," answered Daw casually, as if he was used to selling such luxurious products. "After all, our friend Bruce here still has some underworld contacts. Right?"

"You know me, Daw. You really do."

Chapter 15

After finding such delight from kayaking the previous day, the husband and wife had camped overnight beside the water and continued their river excursion the following morning. Lucille had quickly tired of the monotonous paddling and left Justin to do the heavy lifting while she pointed out multitudes of species in every direction she looked.

"Look, Justin, a piranha!" cried Lucille consulting one of the many thick field guides beside her.

"What species is it?" asked Justin, stopping the kayak for a well-deserved rest that he was glad to find an excuse for.

"It's a red-bellied!"

"That's nice, honey."

But Lucille had been quick to notice the droop in his shoulders just as she noticed field marks with pinpoint accuracy on animals.

"I think we can turn back now; we'll see more that way," she decided.

Justin paddled back toward the trail leading to where they rented the kayak, fueled with new determination and a lucky gust of tailwind. Lucille helped paddle, too and, hiking briskly, they reached the tourist accommodations in less time than it had taken them to get to the river.

The first thing they immediately noticed was emptiness. All of the housing was still there, but there were no more people. All of the small smiling faces were gone. But the tour guide greeted them like everything was normal and took back the kayak, giving the couple back their IDs, until Justin spotted the blood on the ground.

It was a sickening sight, like the death was recent and he knew he hadn't seen it before. He was confident that whatever it was, had been done by a gun, as the gunpowder residue could be both seen and smelled. There were other nauseating colored fluids mixed in with the blood, and some strips of flesh and muscle remained. And he could just make out the majestic pattern of the jaguar, bloodstained and torn.

"What is that?" he asked tentatively, turning around to face the tour guide, and holding a finger toward the sight.

His wife looked surprised, but he could detect the traces of fear and obvious sheepishness on the tour guide's face.

"I don't know what you mean..."

By this point, Lucille had followed her husband's finger and seen the jaguar remains as well. She was enraged.

"You know exactly what he means," Lucile spat, taking an angry step toward the tour guide, making him instinctively throw his hands over his head.

"Well, see here, you have no right to be accusing me of such things."

"There is a dead jaguar in your tour accommodations here. I'd say we have every right and just as much responsibility to call the authorities,`` she replied through her teeth.

"Oh, the authorities already came and a really haughty man took the pelt for disposal," said the tour guide, acting like it had been all his idea. "So I'll tell you again to stop pestering me and get out of my sight."

The couple walked away, Lucille stomping infuriatedly, like a child throwing a tantrum. They set up camp in a clearing nearby and after preparing the tent, both husband and wife flopped inside, needing rest, even while it was the middle of the day.

"We need to do something," said Lucille.

“I know, but what are we supposed to do against some big tour corporation? We have no power here. Our purpose is research for the rainforest, and we have more than enough data now,” replied Justin.

“I want to do something more.”

Chapter 16

Eating fish like he had been doing before, the river dolphin reasoned that he should at least enjoy this new place while he could. The chances were in favor of him dying soon, so he wanted to enjoy what he could before meeting his end.

He had listened to the other pod, though, and stayed away from things he did not know, like the massive fish and the large ruins that the dolphin longed to explore. Instead, he had taken out his feelings on the fish he hunted and ate lots more than he ever had to quench his everlasting hunger, which was really just boredom in another form.

Instead of swimming in the main river that he thought was the vast Amazon, he had floated into a smaller river that he was certain would later connect back. There, yet again, visible through the murky waters of the tributary was the finless, tailless fish that had killed the lizard earlier. He propelled his tail backward and swum away from this creature, while maintaining eye contact the entire time. As the dolphin swam in reverse through the tributary, he approached the ruins, doing all that was in his conscious control not to venture into the shallow stream that led even closer to the mystical building.

However, by the ruins, a lone human was digging with a large object, scooping out the brown earth from the ground and onto a pile of dirt. A large, white tent stood near the scene. As he drifted toward it, his skin detected a prickly sensation, and he sensed a thin fish-like creature sending off electrical pulses. The river dolphin twisted his body around and swam away from that too, not wanting to feel the full strength of the small creature, even though he didn't know exactly what it could do. But he was wise to flee, as the animal had been an electric eel, holding the power to discharge hundreds of volts of electricity into the water with the flick of a tail.

As he joined back into the main river, he left behind the human as well, forgotten. But the human had been one of many archeologists throughout the rainforest, excavating the ruins to find what secrets they hid. However, it was of no importance to the river dolphin and rightfully so, for he struggled to survive in his unforgiving environment, whereas the human had all he needed and was bothered by mosquito bites, not starvation.

He drifted carelessly now, listening to the distant crash of the waterfall and chirping birds and insects with their consistent rhythms and trills piercing the air one after another. But soon, he was swimming and rotating his neck entirely around to stir up crabs and shrimp to feed on. He found nothing, however, as he turned around to head toward the waterfall, a delicious meal was floating in front of him, just waiting to be eaten.

Floating upside down, the river dolphin snuck up underneath his prey and slammed his snout upward, using his very flexible neck to aid him with the spearing motion. The limp body that lay upside-down was none other than a turtle, knocked out cold by the force of the blow. He swam it to shore and began to eat, picking at the insides that were unprotected by the shell.

Night was falling, not that it made much difference to the dark, murky waters that the dolphin swam in, but other animals were resting and some were just beginning to come out. So, the river dolphin lay still, preparing for rest through the night.

***

Along with her mate, the monkey had been spared from the falling trees, but her mother had not made it through. They had tried to take her body, but strong branches fell, pinning it down and eventually, a tree flattened the body, spurting the little blood left inside up into the air. But the monkeys had no time to act, for more trees were falling, so they fled to safety. When night came, they did not get peace at all and were glad for the morning to come.

A pack of female coatis in a nearby tree was whooping in despair at the destruction of their home, and the death of some of their companions only added to the overall heartbreak. How the two mates longed for a troop that would care for them in these struggles. Being alone was a harsh punishment for their species as loneliness easily affected their delicate hearts. The trees that were held dearly in the souls of so many of the animals of this jungle were simply diced into logs by the humans that cut them.

"If you'll be chopping the trees around here, I don't want this many dead animals to clean up," a large man criticized, noticing the mix of animal corpses that littered the barren jungle floor, "These big ones are a pain to get rid of, and they're completely worthless!" he continued in dismay, observing the dead coatis.

"Well," said another man, "I'm sure someone can hook you up,"

"Who would you recommend, huh, Daw?" the large person asked in an exasperated tone.

"Turns out he's right here," Daw responded. He pointed a finger at the man who had been previously boasting about his escapade in the Chinese mountains.

Bruce slapped Daw on the back in a friendly manner and said, "Now don't get me all caught up in your black market exploits... I'm just providing some contacts, that's all."

Meanwhile, the monkeys were contemplating whether to stay or leave. Staying could result in their deaths, but going away could leave them starving and depressed, as territorial animals patrolled all the other areas. The male did not believe, for a second, that humans were as kind as the monkey told him, but went along with it anyway, compassionate as he was. In the end, the two decided to move farther into the forest, still staying near the area so they had readily available sources of food and water, with a familiar habitat surrounding them.

They turned tail and left the trees that had sheltered them, knowing that these would be the next to fall. Off the two mates went, choosing life over death and leaving the spirit of the female's mother behind them.

Chapter 17

Dr. Jacobson prepared the team for another testing of the floodgates and valves. The group needed all of them operational, but so far, only some had been tested. Opening all of them at once would prove dangerous for the river and would flood it too much, so the workers needed to be cautious in how they ran their trials.

"Jessica, can you have Damien work the controls this time? We need to have everyone comfortable with the process in the case of a future emergency," Dr. Jacobson dictated.

"Of course, Ma'am," was Jessica's disciplined reply, just as dedicated to the project as her boss. She approached a man wearing an identical vest and construction hat. "Damien, you're running it this time."

"Okay, let's do this!" he said enthusiastically.

"Open floodgate four in three, two, one, now!"

Right on Jessica's cue, the gate holding back the water opened and the impact was immediately noticeable.

The river surged and water rose from the ground, reaching up to the workers' knees and spreading outward.

"Close the gates! You opened another one as well!" called one of the workers to Damien,

"Already on it."

The temporary scare of flooding was gone, soon absorbed into the currently muddy ground and fast-flowing river.

"It's okay, everyone. Accidents happen and now we know what we need to fix," Dr. Jacobson told everyone, while jotting down the issue on her clipboard. "Floodgate four should open independently, so get to work on that. And excellent work, Zack, for seeing what the problem was. You're running the test next time."

"Yes, Ma'am."

The workers went to fix the problem, but far along up the river, the river dolphin awoke to the sudden gush of water and flooding. He was pushed into a tree and struggled to maintain control when the river became a raging torrent and pulled him along, barely managing to escape to safety into a smaller stream nearby.

***

"If I ever see that filthy tour guide again, I'll–"

"Do what? What exactly do you plan to do?" demanded Justin, cutting off Lucille.

"You mean to tell me that I don't really care?" Lucille challenged.

"All I mean to tell you is that you can't do anything about it. Just let it go. At the beginning of this trip, you told me to relax."

"Oh, so now you're going to use that against me?" she replied harshly.

"I'm not using anything against you. Give me a solid plan and I'll support you all the way, but this is getting both of us nowhere."

Lucille paused a moment before her reply: "Okay. Okay. We will take a picture of these remains for now. We can ask the tour guide to narrate what occurred and that will be broadcast on television. We will bring him to the city, and–"

"Hold on," said Justin, cutting her off again, "First of all, he told us never to show our faces there again. Second, he won't tell us a thing. And third, he already told the authorities! Think your way through this; we can't just try random things!"

"So why don't we ask one of the residents of the cabin? They'll be out and about today, since I'm pretty sure there's nothing planned by that guide. They can narrate the incident."

"They were all gone! Didn't you see how empty the place looked?"

"Then we will wait to talk to them! They have to return to their rooms eventually, so when they enter the area, we pull one person over, and ask if they saw the killing."

"They left, Lucille! The tourists are gone."

"You don't know that. Where have they gone? Simply vaporized into thin air?"

"What I do know is that you are hopeless," Justin sighed, rubbing his temples.

***

The river dolphin was still shocked by the sudden changes in the water and decided to hunt, but it seemed that almost all of the fish had been swept downriver by the current. The few remaining had escaped into small hiding places that the river dolphin would have to work hard to find. He moved his tail up and down, propelling his streamlined body forward and came upon an animal just as big as him. But the newcomer was not a river dolphin. By contrast, he had rich brown fur that insulated his body from water, and he twisted gracefully in the water using large, webbed paws and a stout tail. This new animal was an otter, also looking for fish after the water levels' turbulent changes.

Unlike the river dolphin, the otter was not alone but swam with other members of his kind, all trying to fill their significant needs of. Heeding the other river dolphins' advice, the river dolphin stayed away, watching from a distance out of curiosity, letting the otters swim and rest on the banks of the creek they had claimed as home. Soon, the dolphin learned he was right to stay away after noticing deep gashes in a fallen tree on which the otters rested. The size and depth of the marks matched the otters' claws and teeth, which added to the intimidation already present from the animals' size.

One of the hiding fish now ventured slowly out from the roots of a sunken tree and an otter was immediately upon it, catching the fish in his mouth as the body flopped dead from the impact of sharp claws. It was so quick and powerful that the river dolphin did not dare compete with these creatures for food, as he knew he would likely lose anyway, although his agility and compatibility with the water were equally formidable.

Soon, the diversity of animals evened out as different species mingled between ecosystems and the balance between predators and prey got one step closer to how it was before. However, the dolphin was thinking of how the other river dolphins had their pod and how the otters had their family, while he was left with nothing. The excitement that this new place brought him was constantly blighted by loneliness.

Chapter 18

After running from the humans and their metal beasts, the monkeys found guavas, savoring the sweet juices that streamed down their faces and into their mouths. The two stuffed themselves full of the seeded pink flesh and their excrement spread seeds of the fruit like their ancestors had to preserve the forest and make it what it was at that time. But it seemed that even though they were actively dispersing seeds from their food, their efforts were futile as the humans could destroy the saplings that would sprout with utmost ease.

After eating, the monkeys teased each other, taunting with their body language and making a variety of vocalizations. Eventually, they ended up wrestling in a playful tangle and hung from branches with their tails while still play-fighting. The male pulled the female closer on a branch after a while and wrapped his arms around her, showing affection, and she hugged him in return, glad to have someone in her life she could rely on. They lay there in a shaded spot, and as the male caressed his mate's back like the humans had done before, she drifted off. Soon the male followed her, napping in the warm afternoon sun.

The two monkeys woke to a blowing wind that was only felt because the humans had taken so much of the forest that protected them. Heeding the pangs of hunger in their stomachs, the monkeys gathered seeds and more guavas to feast upon. From their secluded spot on the canopy of the tall tree, they observed the forest around them, which, little known to them, would be whittled down to a far smaller range, turned into trivial human accessories like paper, cosmetics, and varnish.

For now, they were living in the moment, experiencing the forest how it was and not how it would be. Save for a single barren patch, the entire forest was filled densely with tall, majestic spires of wood and leaves, or so they thought. They were limited by how far they were willing to travel and the two monkeys had no idea how many humans had easy access to the rainforest and were killing it every second. It was facile for them to think they might be unaffected, as they did not consider how much humans had already taken from them. So they munched away on their food in peace, the female still disoriented about the human species after the woman had saved her from a very certain death. But the disdain with which the male observed the barren spot caught the eye of the female. She wondered why he didn't see it as just a little patch of the rainforest reserved for the humans, who were so kind and caring.

***

"Lucille!" Justin yelled, chasing after the sobbing woman that was running away from him, "Please, listen to me!"

After he insulted her in the tent, tears of anger had welled up in her eyes and she had taken off with the single-minded goal of getting away from whom she considered the inconsiderate man that had charmed her into marrying him. Now he chased after her, trying to get her to listen to reason, but she did not want to. She wanted someone to speak up for all of the deaths that had gone over the world's heads in the name of progress, superiority, or even for the greater good. She needed justice to be brought to the animals and environment of Earth. In her mind, she planned to do something about the planet's destruction, with or without Justin's help.

But to keep her from seeing how different they both truly were, Justin claimed he wanted her goals just as much as her, only without the desperation and sadness she created. He made a last-ditch attempt to please his angered wife when dialing a number to receive a jeep ride to the city nearby for her to take any further steps she wanted. Of course, the vehicle would not enter the rainforest, so the two had to go to it. However, for that to happen, his wife would need to calm her easily-agitated self down.

Lucille was too tired to keep running and sat behind a tree so Justin would not be able to see her weeping face, blotchy with red spots. Justin could hear her sobs and came slowly, as one would do when approaching a wounded animal to help it. His knees were bent and exhaustion was evident on his face, but he still tried to make peace.

"Honey... I've called for a jeep to pick us up. We can go to the city and do something there." Lucille acted as if she had gone temporarily deaf and stopped crying, putting on a grim outward form. However, Justin had not given up hope yet, "Well, it's a shame that humans cannot understand animals," he began. But Lucille still did not acknowledge his appearance, "but now your beautiful voice can speak for them, and I can never get tired of hearing it."

Now she finally looked at her husband, chuckling between sobs that had started once more. She held out her hand and Justin willingly held it tightly in his.

Together, they gathered their equipment, truly following the unwritten rule between all who loved nature: 'leave only footprints, take only memories.' When heading toward the jeep's location, all was forgiven and they passed by the site of the loggers, disdainfully observing their camp.

"That's just another thing that we'll have to fix," said Justin, not only for his wife's benefit, but for his own. Though he didn't act it, the people destroying the rainforest with their every action gave him pain too, and regret for being part of such a self-absorbed species. Then there came the unmistakable squelch of flesh on a boot.

"Oops!" a stocky man said sarcastically, observing the stain on his sole. He was one of the people working to chop down the forest and his colleagues chuckled along with him at the dead animal he had mockingly stepped on.

Near the edges of the camp were men with chainsaws cutting trees ruthlessly. As the couple scanned the entire scene, they were both revolted by the actions of the humans.

Chapter 19

Seeking to find fish of his own, the river dolphin swam around rocks and dead tree stumps at the bottom of the dark water, sensing objects around him with his specialized form of echolocation adapted for use underwater. He tracked down a school of shrimp and streaked through them, catching many in his mouth while the others scurried away.

Satisfied for now, the river dolphin returned to watch the otters, who were darting around each other playfully and floating on their backs. The sight brought another pang to his heart, as he and his sister used to do the exact same thing. He wondered why this family of otters was so much like his pod. But they were not fearful like his parents and other family. Perhaps the otters were mistaken there, but the river dolphin did not suspect that in the least.

Another otter popped up from below the water's surface with one more catch of fish. However, after he ate the fish, he went ashore to rest and began acting strangely. The river dolphin saw the otter walk in circles and fall over, which he had never seen an otter do before. Then the otter rushed to the bank of the creek he was in and dug frantically, until a canoe approached from a connecting stream.

The otter rushed toward it, which he would never have done in a typical scenario, while the other otters hid, bewildered by their family member's actions. However, the river dolphin knew what was happening only too well. He had seen the same happenings after his uncle had eaten a catfish before his pod had relocated for the first time, so he knew that the strangely acting otter had ingested too much mercury. It was a cumulative process, from everything the otter ate, that stemmed from the gold miners and the river dolphin was surprised that he hadn't seen this occur sooner. If the archeologist that he had seen was here, there were bound to be gold miners that used their chemicals to separate their precious ore from the mud. And then, because they didn't want to risk contact with mercury, the miners burned it off their metal and released it into the air for animals of the rainforest to eat. Of course, biomagnification took its toll and now, the otter had too much mercury in his liver, resulting in his surely imminent killing.

The otter approached the vessel with much less grace than he had demonstrated before, swimming haphazardly and making many splashes that alerted the man in the boat to the otter. The man showed apparent interest in the otter, but the look on his face was one of vengeance. After casting a fishing net that would deplete food sources here and give him mercury poisoning, too, he picked up an airgun from the floor of his craft. The otter lay on his back, exposing his soft underside to the man, who, without hesitation, fired his airgun, a shot to where the otter's head connected to his body that stained the white patterns on his neck brutally red.

"Ha!" the man whooped. "Now you can't steal my fish anymore."

***

Raising her head in the sky, the monkey smelled something sweet in the air, almost too sweet, and motioned for her mate to sniff for the aroma as well. He could smell it, too, and his eyes grew wide as he realized where he had recognized it from. He told his mate about the rare delicacy they were smelling and how he had only eaten it once before, triggering a memory in the monkey's mind. She remembered now when her troop had talked wistfully about the food known as honey, guarded by swarming insects that painfully stung their skin. Only a few members in her troop had ever had the sweet, syrupy luxury when they had, by some stroke of luck, come upon a fallen hive. But even then, it was rare to find it unclaimed by another animal that wanted it just as much.

The monkeys followed their noses to the scent and it was already claimed, but not by other monkeys, which they stood no chance against. Instead, a skunk was munching on chunks of honeycomb and the scent wafted up through the trees, making the two monkeys' mouths water.

Both of the mates had come across skunks before in their respective lives and knew that the odor of the spray would mask the honey's sweetness and bring ruin to their sensitive eyes and noses. Taking caution, they scaled the tree, rustling branches and hoping the sound would seem like a bird in the branches so they could derive benefit from the skunk's greatest fear of owls. Owls had no sense of smell, giving the skunks in the Amazon no defense against the birds. This made spraying useless, so their only option was to run away in terror.

The plan succeeded thus far as the skunk froze, staring with its beady eyes up at the sky. Beginning to caterwaul with hoots and howls, the monkey's sounds resembled those of the owls in residence nearby. The fearsome sounds were the final straw for the skunk, and he bolted off in terror, leaving an entire section of the honeycomb untouched for the cunning monkeys.

Descending rapidly, the two monkeys were glad to see none of the stinging creatures in sight and broke off large chunks of their well-earned treat, feeding each other by smothering each other's faces with the sticky substance that tasted like pure joy. It was a lucky find that completely slowed down the monkeys' usually frantic brains with pure relaxation as if the gooey honey had coated it as well.

Chapter 20

The couple took their time taking photos of all the aspects of the deforestation site, especially of the burning fires that were surely illegal. Both husband and wife seriously doubted that the permits and paperwork that the people had were authentic, even as they had managed to forge multiple ID cards, without anyone noticing, that read, '100% authentic.'

Suddenly, the two heard the cries of a baby caracara who was unable to fly, still in a nest. The parents of the bird flew to their child's aid, dive-bombing the people cutting the tree, but they had futile effects against the strength of the construction hats that the humans wore and were warded off by the chainsaw-commanding people.

Justin took a step forward, knowing that trying to help the birds was a guaranteed way to re-win his wife's trust in him. But Lucille grabbed his upper arm to hold him back, fearful of the sawing machines that the men carried.

She looked at him quizzically, "Didn't you tell me that we have no power against big corporations?"

"We don't. Saving that bird will not do anything at all. In fact, these people will just kill ten more. But I am not going to stand by and let this happen. Even though it won't change a thing."

In truth, he just wanted to prove to his wife that helping nature was important to him too.

Fueled by pure desperation and love, Justin wrenched his arm free of her grasp and ran toward the men cutting the trees, calling at them to stop, while his wife watched, paralyzed by fear. The men turned in surprise, wondering whom the shouts were coming from, holding their chainsaws up just as the tree fell.

One of the people called for help from their boss, Daw, and began interrogating Justin on the spot. But he paid the loggers no heed as the baby bird fell, even as they wielded their deadly weapons.

The adult caracaras ferociously attacked Justin, not realizing that he was trying to help and only seeing an attacker they could harm. Their powerful talons and keratin beaks tore into his forearms and face, but his concentration was enough to save the baby and let it be carried away to safety. Bleeding and successful, he turned back to the surprised loggers as the man named Daw strode toward him.

"What do you think you're doing? Are you out of your mind?" demanded Daw. "My friends here are working hard to provide your lives with quality wood products, and you are trying to get yourself killed while they work an honest but demanding job."

"Well, I'm trying to save a poor helpless baby and provide it with a better future. It's an honest but demanding job," Justin replied, mocking the logger's words.

"The company I work for has bought this land and has every right to kick you off, so be glad I'm not pressing charges. And leave here immediately."

Justin listened and retreated to his wife, satisfied that he was able to get to the man named Daw. Then smirking, he said to his wife, "I just had the weirdest thought. Imagine these trees started bleeding, then they would be in for a surprise."

"How can you be so casual? You could have been killed! And there is a tree that can bleed. It's called the Socotra Dragon Tree, native to an archipelago in the Arabian Sea and…" Lucille trailed off, realizing how easily she had gotten distracted. Pulling out cloth patches from her seemingly bottomless backpack, she applied pressure on Justin's wounds and taped some of the material down to quell the bleeding.

"Leave it to you to know something like that off the top of your head," Justin laughed and took her by the hand toward their waiting ride to the city, which sounded so welcoming now.

***

"Are we ready for the next test?" Jessica asked the technicians of the dam.

"Yes, we have been able to fix the problem and we're ready to test floodgate four again," one person replied.

"Zack, you know how everything works?" called Jessica to the man scheduled to run the test that time around.

"Ready as I'll ever be," came the confident answer.

"Okay, let's do this one more time, open the floodgate in…" she gave her countdown and all of the systems worked perfectly, leaving only a few more tests before the turbines would begin to turn the force of the Amazon River into a sustainable and reliable energy source.

As Jessica oversaw the testing like usual, Dr. Jacobson conversed with a formally dressed man, who had a small hiking pack on his back.

"You've checked the environmental impacts of this project?" she asked him.

"I have. There are no effects on the amazing biodiversity here, in fact, occasional flooding could help river dolphins with travel and trees with their cooling systems," the man assured her.

"You've researched this thoroughly?" she queried.

"Well, yes! Yes, I have," he guaranteed, but, though the doctor didn't hear it, the slight hesitation in his voice gave away the lie he had told to keep his pride. He continued by saying, "Seeing the impacts of projects like this poses many difficulties and even professionals don't have enough evidence to prove anything. However, I am sure everything will be fine."

Although he did have the Amazon's best interest in mind, enough research was not available about the direct influences of the hydroelectric dam on the river and forest inhabitants.

Unfortunately, Dr. Jacobson gave him the benefit of the doubt.

Meanwhile, the workers waited for the river to settle so they could test the final two floodgates without causing a flood like the one before. They were able to run another successful test before it was called a day and darkness crept through the luminescent skies, transitioning the land from day to night.

Chapter 21

The shocked river dolphin watched as the gleeful man lifted the limp body of the otter out of the water, a red tinge remaining in the place where he last lay in the river. However, the river dolphin knew this scene all too well. He had lost his uncle in a similar tragic manner too, the same slow, painful death from mercury poisoning that left him lifeless in the water, only to later be picked up by humans greedily desiring his organs and meat to spread as bait for fish. It brought him no solace to think that the otter would be killed either way, as both deaths still stemmed from the humans. The dead otter was hauled from the murky river into the waiting hands of the hunter, taken back to the craft in which man had arrived. There, the human cut open his kill with a knife and skinned it, leaving the entrails of the otter to lure in the day's expected catch.

"I can take you home, and we will make so much money together. I think that should be enough payment for the fish that you stole from me," the human cackled in a deranged manner and paddled away, leaving his cast net behind to catch unsuspecting animals that failed to sense the ghostly presence of it.

The dramatic event of the otter's death had taken the complete focus of the river dolphin and he failed to notice another change in the flow of the river, not as conspicuous as before, but still a noticeable change to others nearby.

Meanwhile, the otters mourned, paddling to the sight of their family member's death and recovering tufts of fur. At this sight, the dolphin nostalgically remembered yet again how his pod had reacted to his uncle's sudden, unprecedented death that had been foreshadowed only in subtle, undetectable ways.

The otters caught more fish and lay them near the collected fur and skin, not eating themselves, but crying out in obvious pain and trauma. Their playful river dolphin-like spirits were crushed and they went into their den, full of sadness, not at all the sociable creatures they used to be. Silence now filled their dwelling and they stared into empty space, lost and heartbroken, while suffering physically from their distress by not eating. And the river dolphin could not help but feel the same way as the otters, for the experience was so similar to him and he had felt like part of their family even though, of course, he was truly all alone.

***

The monkeys lounged about the dirt floor of the Amazon under the foliage that protected them from the glaring sun. The broken honeycombs from which the monkeys had devoured the sweet honey were now spreading their aroma, beckoning other hungry animals to come and consume it. The first animal to steal bits of their meal was another skunk who had been slinking about in the undergrowth. It took a small piece from below the monkey's distracted eyes, but even if they had noticed, they had eaten enough to be satisfied. However, the next animal that wanted a part of the delicious meal was a bullet ant and along with others of its rank, marching in a steady line toward the honey.

One crawled over the monkeys' fur and the male was aroused with a start, crushing the ant beneath his paw and staring with horror at the army that was seizing their honey. He alerted his mate, and they realized the time had come to leave their treat to the jungle, avoiding the deadly, painful sting these ants could give. As they headed back to their tree, they observed the multitude of animals the honey had now attracted, all squabbling amongst themselves. The monkeys could only think how fortunate they were to have received the treat so readily, though it was also due to their intellect and not just luck.

From the dense layers of trees that formed a curtain between the unexplored jungle and the humans' clearing, a thundering noise erupted. It was followed by the startled squawks of the avian inhabitants, whose homes were getting demolished. Then came the buzzing that turned a tree into timber, the eventual use of which would be decided by those who cut it for their profit and nothing more. Not for a family, not for food, and definitely not for the sustenance of life, as all of the forest creatures used the trees for.

From far above the canopy came an odd whirring noise and the beating of wind from above. The female knew it was one of the kind humans' contraptions they possibly used to save animals. Although this caught the interest of the monkeys, it was to the dismay of the loggers.

"Hey! Level 2 lockdown in process! Everyone hide in the tents, and take any handheld equipment with you! Daw, hide that jaguar and prepare our permits and such," a man yelled from within his horde of workers. Other men piloting large machines drove them into the forest, now somewhat out of sight, but quite visible to those who gave closer inspection. However, the helicopter only landed in the open clearing and was apparently satisfied seeing the permits that read '100% authentic' like people's ID cards after taking an amount of money more extensive than most of the loggers' yearly salary.

"Well, although the Amazon is notorious for its illegal poaching activity and such, here we have some law-abiding citizens who have lawfully purchased land and are putting it to best-permitted use, legally clearing space with controlled fires. Keep up the good work, men!" the soldier who stepped out from the helicopter reported, observing the paperwork of the men. His words were bitterly sarcastic, as, unlike the many attempting to protect the forest, he was willing to turn a blind eye to illegal activity for money. And, to anyone who asked, he would claim that these loggers were part of a perfectly legal company that rightfully bought and deserved this land.

Chapter 22

Lucille and Justin arrived at the waiting vehicle later than expected, but Justin tipped the driver extra as compensation for the delay. The driver gave a grateful smile and helped them load their luggage before turning the jeep onto a dirt road and flooring the gas pedal, making the engine roar.

"I received the destination in your text after you called me. You two want to go back here, right?" the driver confirmed, showing an address on his phone. The two gave a nod and began talking amongst themselves. From the edge of the rainforest where they had been picked up, they merged onto a freeway that would lead them to their desired destination.

As the car rumbled along the freeway, they observed glimpses of animals that, sadly, were desperate enough to approach the human roads. It was about an hour's drive to the city and the entire time, Lucille was thinking about how the humans were demolishing the beautiful rainforest they had been sent to for research. She and her husband had collected more than enough recounts of interspecies interactions and such, but in her opinion, not nearly enough about conservation and protection.

"So do you think we should head to the company building first or do you have some other plan?" asked Justin.

"I think we should tell the other researchers about it and someone will know what to do. No sense in heading straight to the authorities and just telling them that they are horrible at what they're supposed to do," Lucille told him.

"I agree. But this is our first research project in the Amazon and everyone's still getting used to everything after our previous location up north. It was the complete opposite of here and we should give the team time to adjust as well," suggested Justin.

They arrived at the building that they had departed from for their journey, the day seeming so long ago. It was a welcoming place with ebony doors that blended into a wide building, walled in a smooth, dark material. The area was floored with black marbled tile and had large, darkened windows that let in the perfect amount of light to focus. Colleagues peeked their heads through their respective doors to welcome the returning couple.

Both of them headed straight toward what seemed to be the main office and were greeted by a man behind his desk. The man folded down his laptop screen and smiled.

"Welcome back! I hope everything went well for you?" he asked, although it was more of a statement than a question.

Justin squeezed Lucille's hand in warning and responded, "It was a wondrous adventure, sir, and we both enjoyed it thoroughly. We look forward to comparing our observations to the results of the team's predictions soon, but we also both had some concerns we wanted to address. So, if we could talk to you whenever you're available, that would be great."

"Yes, feel free to talk to me, perhaps tomorrow sometime. I'll get back to you on that. However, please make yourselves comfortable with your colleagues for now and relax. You've probably done a wonderful job of research, as your previous expeditions have shown and everything can wait."

"Okay, I suppose it all can wait," said Lucille, "And it really was a marvelous experience out there in the wilderness, just like all the times before."

***

The river dolphin had followed another tributary downstream to find crabs and other crustaceans. He knew, now, that he could be just as close as the otter to a death like that, driven to madness and finally killed. After leaving the site of the otter's death, he had simply floated, detached from the animals he had connected to in a mental sense of being and still forever lost from his true family.

Thinking about the delicious fish that he enjoyed daily, the river dolphin knew that all of his prey in the river would have concentrations of poison, but he thought that satiating himself on smaller creatures may give him a lower rate of mortality. Yet somehow, the river was becoming less populated with prey and, while there was still enough for the river dolphin, it was an odd revelation after years of having an unlimited food supply with his pod.

He knew that other animals, including some of the otters he encountered previously, would vie for the remaining fish, too, leaving him with more challenges to face during his coming searches for food. For the time being, he was able to snag a few shrimp between his jaws, though he only ate his fill and no more than he truly needed.

Reminiscing about the old times with his sister, he remembered when they had chased each other around with grasses and sticks that they had later tossed around and terrified small striped snakes along the water's edge. Almost subconsciously, the river dolphin dove down and pulled up grasses as he had with their sister, making his memories more clear and vivid, this time scaring away a squirrel drinking water from the riverbank when the grasses went flying in an arch above him with the jerk of his neck. It felt so natural to feel the love that he had not felt for so long, but it all vanished instantly, along with his other recollections, as he realized, again, that things would never be the same.

Chapter 23

Other than the calling of birds and the music of bugs, there was silence. It was so sharp and clear that the monkey realized how much noise the humans had created, tuned out by her ears after the initial pain that it caused in her youth. The sudden stop of noise brought a new sense of wonder to the entire forest, with melodies that could be heard at last, but only by those that truly listened. The soft thump, as the two mates jumped onto the soft ground, seemed to echo and they slowed down their gait upon entering a clearing, where they looked up at the forest with new eyes. For once, the trees they appreciated were not meeting tragic deaths by the second and could be admired without the fear of their falling.

But the humans did not care about preservation. The helicopter had left mere minutes ago and, already, the loggers were preparing to get back to work. And the forest creatures could tell what was happening, as men approached, welding metal-toothed chainsaws and silencing animals even from meters away.

Soon, the tumult was back, though. By instinct, the monkey tuned it out, at the cost of losing the hidden notes that the jungle had sung for a fragment of time. They were now a mere memory.

The mates retreated to the trees to eat leaves, eying the skies warily due to the scarcity of foliage above them. However, the two monkeys had noticed that the population of raptors had been steadily decreasing.

Whether that was a good sign or bad, they could not tell, though they stayed cautious, nevertheless.

Meanwhile, a monkey troop of another species was approaching, and his ears picked up the sound, alerting him to the trouble that surely would follow if the two were to stay. Quickly, he warned his mate and they took to the branches, gracefully escaping the harsh consequences that could have been received otherwise. The monkey knew that the social hierarchy was needed, however. It just felt unfair to be so alone because of her mistakes, even though, in reality, only the humans were to blame.

***

"There were birds and insects, lizards and frogs on every tree; I spotted quite a few new species for myself and uncommon ones in the area," Lucille told a group of people, speaking animatedly.

In another room, Justin was having a similar experience as his stories captivated the attention of just as many people.

"We were looking for some carnivorous plants, and we found one, all right! There was a sundew! That far south and not even at that high of an elevation. Can you even believe it?"

And all while the memories were being shared, fingers flew across keyboards, tapping frantically and adding information that only experienced researchers were able to find and interpret accurately. New trends were in the process of being discovered and it took the team's combined efforts for the statistics to help support protection for the incredible place that directly supported human lives worldwide. But to Lucille, something felt missing. She knew that they had helped, she knew that she should be grateful, yet she wanted to do more. After all they had seen and felt, it seemed like she needed to give something back to the rainforest that so many animals called home.

As Lucille contemplated what the wildlife deserved in her head, she remembered all of her other expeditions as well, in places just as wonderful. Now she was not as naive as she had been before, though, and knew that helping the Amazon would only fill part of the emptiness that she felt. A significant amount, but not nearly enough.

As Justin finalized the research results with his team, he was thinking along the same lines as Lucille. He had always loved her bold personality, but she seemed a little extreme to him during the trip. She had the right idea in mind, but he felt certain that she was taking it too far. Of course, he wanted to support her, but compromise, not blindly following her, was the best solution he could think of. However, a voice in the back of his head kept him in conflict.

"Whether she's right or wrong, I just don't want to lose her," he muttered.

"What?" asked a colleague squinting at papers and sitting beside him.

"Hm? Oh. Um... nothing?" Justin replied awkwardly.

***

Jessica paced, impatient for the dam to become fully functional. Embarking on a project like this had been her lifelong dream after seeing the effects of climate change firsthand. While she was still in college, a hurricane swept in from the Atlantic Ocean and took thousands of lives, including those of her parents. It had been the same year that she was majoring in environmental science, and while the sadness took the purpose of life away from her, she knew it was not uncontrollable like some were trying to convince her, and that increased hurricane strengths and frequencies were due to the unruly abuse that humans had given the atmosphere with greenhouse gas emissions.

Many of the workers for the dam didn't share similar backgrounds with her, but also wanted cleaner energy from more renewable sources. Dr. Jacobson, for example, had led multiple teams before, heading projects for solar and wind farms. She had succeeded, but not nearly enough to make a dent in rising temperatures.

While multiple tests were being conducted, most people at the site were checking that the main parts of the dam, turbines and generators, worked to the full capacity and were constantly reliable. Others worked to start the flow of the dam without disrupting the water levels that were in check from the extra pathways they had excavated. Water entered and rotated the turbines, transforming the kinetic energy into electricity at an impressive rate, due to the strength of the mighty river. As it all exited from the tailrace, the operators of the dam rushed to stem the flow of the reservoir's liquid and let the river return to its natural state. Relief was brought to many stressed minds as a result of their success. After almost two decades of work, they were so close now.

Chapter 24

The sound of grinding accompanied wood chips flying into the sky as men lugged stray logs and branches into a wood chipper. Soil was constantly eroded as once-forested land was cleared. Dust and dirt flew into the eyes and mouths of people, making them cough forcefully. Meanwhile, the small fires with the original purpose of flattening the ground were now even bigger, decimating larger areas of land by the second. One of the loggers had struck a deal with a commercial farmer who offered to pay big money for a spacious, entirely cleared piece of land in the rainforest. He was discovered forging land ownership papers by leaders of the logging company, who immediately bought into the opportunity, bribing the man who had made the deal with future prospects for money in exchange for receiving a portion of cash from the farmer.

Not all working at the site were so heartless, however, and some even felt sorrow at seeing so much life meet an untimely end, but they needed the money and if illegal work was the easiest way, it did not matter to them. Of course, the most pervasive justification was that none of what they were doing actually mattered because there were plenty of rainforests and animals in the world. If not, humans were the dominant species and such destruction wouldn't affect them. Not a single person aiding in the deforestation came close to realizing how wrong these justifications were.

Gary, instead of taking pride in mocking more dead animals, was helping cut through a particularly dense group of flowers, trees, and other plants, resorting to brutal stabs with his chainsaw, alongside fellow workers. As usual, he had sunk to using brute force, rather than utilizing the minuscule bit of intellect that he did have, but perhaps that was for the best, so that the jungle could be more resilient and delay its own devastation.

Many other workers were being much more efficient, working much harder than their superiors, while the sun ambled across the sky, even while their share of money was far too small in comparison to be fair. But they were inexplicably loyal, either for the chance at a raise or because of the opportunity at a job without all the strings attached. Gambling, bets, and bribery were commonplace and everyone was looking to dupe and outsmart each other for a bigger chunk of money.

All the forest cared about was providing sanctuary to the creatures within, but it had no defense against these bullies that wreaked havoc. And the more of it that died, the happier the workers were.

***

The river dolphin felt very alone watching a family of capybaras settle nearby for the night. He should have been used to the feeling by now, but years of constant companionship had trained his brain otherwise. Although his primal instinct to hunt came first, he was preserving the food and eating a bare minimal amount due to how low the fish supply had recently gotten.

Because of his sonar, the darkening skies didn't affect him and he was already adapted to the murky water, but many animals retreated to their hiding places, while others came out from theirs. The dolphin didn't feel like sleeping, as he had rested soundly just some time ago. Even with all the other animals that were busy going about their business, the river's wide berth gave each species enough space and the river dolphin faced much less territorial competition here, instead, fighting for the resource of food.

Food for other types of animals wasn't quite the same. As a large rodent tapped logs, locating grubs by the river bank, a lightning-fast bite ended up with a plump snake replacing its position on the wood. In the trees, a kinkajou let out a high pitch squeal and some short chirps that stood out from the mournful birds ever present in sound. The animal flinched in alarm at the snake and eyed it carefully while scooping pulp out of a fig with its tongue. After a moment's apprehension, the kinkajou threw the fig skin at the snake and ducked behind a branch, peering from above to see what would happen.

The snake's entire body twitched and the fig fell harmlessly beside lightning-fast scales, but he became mad and coiled up tightly while hissing. Around it, dozens of kinds of insects appeared and the kinkajou daringly swung down by her tail to catch a few. At the same time, figs higher in the trees attracted bats and nocturnal birds that wanted to join in on the feeding frenzy. Ants had already claimed many of their own feeding locations and swarmed the fruit, covering the green outside with crawling, black bodies. Monkeys screeched from above and the river dolphin experienced it all: the true beauty and wonder of untouched wilderness.

He, too, added to the scene. A sleek, graceful figure that navigated through the water like he was made of air. He twisted and turned, pink skin shining from the moon's reflection in the river stained brown by the tangled mangrove roots and other vegetation that receded into the forest. And for that extraordinary moment, it seemed that this pristine ecosystem, though already facing degeneration from humans, would withstand all to come.

***

"Daw '*Sawdust*' Miller!" the tour guide spat, pacing in circles for one of many nights in a row. "I mean, who does that guy think he is, strutting up to *my* property, taking what was legally *mine* on *my* property, and showing me up in front of my guests?!"

It was uncertain whom the tour guide was trying to convince, but Daw had obviously gotten to him. Of course, all of his customers had soon left after the incident and his ratings were soaring like a rocket... that had badly malfunctioned before exiting the atmosphere and was then ensnared by the pull of gravity. In the tour guide's mind, the man who called himself "Sawdust" had doomed his business for good.

But the tour guide had only been making a substandard profit and not the millions he had hoped for anyways. As of the moment, his financial state was okay because he had been apt enough to have a savings account, but he knew that it would soon be time to start giving things up and wanted to reap any rewards he could. So he made a plan to fire his workers, sell his canoes, and strip the tourist accommodations of everything he had built for a significant chunk of money. From then on, he would have to see what he would do with the empty land.

The tour guide started with the easiest step first, firing his workers.

"So..." he began, "Due to financial issues and such... um... I'm afraid that I will have to fire you all."

It seemed that they were expecting this and simply nodded, proceeding to pack their belongings.

"Of course, you will get paid for an extra month!" the tour guide called cheerfully after them. "You know, until you find a new job and all..."

Chapter 25

"Okay, I've had enough of all this pretending everything is hunky-dory!" Those were the first words Lucille spoke upon waking up later than she had expected and finding everyone poring over research results to make data more readable.

"Because it is not! I refuse to allow such things to happen on my planet and will stand up!" she continued, glaring at the people who were looking at their feet and fidgeting.

Sighing, Justin stood up and led his wife out of the room by her arm. He was used to these instances, what he called "tantrums," but he was always one to avoid a scene and hated making one in front of so many people.

"Listen, honey–" he tried.

"Don't you honey me! You know that it's wrong, don't you?" Lucille's tone softened.

And that was what made it so hard for Justin because he wanted to agree with and support his wife, but at the same time, he didn't want to be involved. He wouldn't do wrong to the environment, but he would stand by and watch it get destroyed.

"There's no one else who will do it. You know that," her voice rose slightly at the end of her sentence, tone reasonable, but pleading as well.

"I do know, but why? Why does it have to be us? Why does no one else care?"

"Oh, Justin, they do care. Some people are afraid, others just accept whatever happens, many simply view humans as the superior species, but the rest? They want to do something because they know that if humans were superior, they would be doing real good, making real change, and taking the first step that only so few are able to take. We have that opportunity, and I will take it, with or without your support."

"Lucille?"

"I love you, Justin, I really do, but what should come first? Answer me honestly. Selfishness and love or the sake of the entire planet along with the future of life as a whole?"

"I don't–" Justin's voice caught.

"It's okay, I understand. This always was the perfect job for you and you are helping in your own way. But I think that I have a different role, the missing piece of the puzzle that would be nothing with the hundreds of other pieces that people like you fit together."

She turned, but, then reconsidering, faced her husband again and pecked him on the lip.

Then Lucille turned on her heel and did what can only be described as gracefully storming off. Justin stood speechless and unsure of what to do or say, wordlessly reaching out after her in utter shock and sadness.

***

Banana peels were already decomposing in the understory as the two monkeys chattered loudly from above, mashing the banana's insides inside their mouth. The sweet flavor rushed endorphins to the two mates' brains and a sense of tranquility fell upon them, along with a sudden covering of clouds. Pattering of rain resounded from the ground up and tree frogs jumped on the chance to boast their presence rather noisily to any females that might be nearby. The tree canopies above collected gallons of water that seemed to form endless streams in the air, perpetually finding gaps in the leaves and branches and crashing down on the now swamp-like forest floor.

Humidity made the two monkeys' fur feel sticky, yet the droplets of water that found their way to their skin felt both refreshing and revitalizing. They both didn't bother to shake the water off their lush fur, knowing that it would dry fast enough after exposure to the sun. It was the same for the towering trees that sucked up tons of water, only to transpire it back into the atmosphere, helping to balance the planet every second. However, this was the most they were able to do, as a plant can only take so many pummelings of excess carbon dioxide intake. And the massive amount of oxygen that this rainforest, "The Lungs of the Earth," produced was only meant to be used on its deserving dwellers, despite supporting a significant percentage of every single human's oxygen induction.

The thunderous gush of the overflowing river fertilized the soils and let animals experience the best of both worlds that the Amazon offered. An iguana propelled itself with its tail into the flooded land as other reptiles, like lizards with bright orange dewlaps, shot up trees, careful to avoid the lurking boas that would roll themselves upon short branches overlooking lower areas.

In elevated places, the torrent was so great that water would skim off the edges to fall and form miniature waterfalls. Off in the distance were mountains and the cascades were large to the extent that they were visible and audible to the two monkeys from some miles of distance, especially with the pulsating rainfall that made them much easier to mentally visualize.

It took a while before the male monkey also realized that the distinct musky odor in the treetops was not solely the warm air and petrichor, but also an animal with dark brown fur sticking out in all directions. He gently showed the female the presence he had just detected, due to the effective camouflage of what they could tell, by the constantly smiling face and streaked eye patches, was a sloth. They didn't mind the sloth's company as the species was one of very gentle and non-threatening creatures. Additionally, it would be an easier target for predators, allowing the monkeys to escape with ease. But neither of the two acknowledged that fact, focusing on the feeling of their hands clasped together, giving each other comfort and assurance that they would always be there by the other's side.

Chapter 26

Near the shore, a fox was looking for crabs, having some success but not much. Nosing along the sandy river bottom, the river dolphin, too, was searching for food and stirred up minuscule crustaceans that it swallowed whole. The creatures that the river dolphin had eaten did barely anything to satisfy his appetite, however. So he used his sonar to its full range while going downstream, clicking loudly and receiving echoes that revealed no bigger prey yet.

The streamlined structure of the river dolphin made his gentle movements, dipping in and out of the water, look like he was effortlessly gliding on the border between the two. He dove down and turned slightly before spinning his body and exploding upward like a cork. As he splashed back down, the satisfying contact with water was paired with the discovery of a large fish up ahead. The river dolphin approached swiftly and the fish got bigger and bigger. First, it was about the size of a piranha, then the size of a satiating meal, and then much too big to be anything good.

The fish ahead began to approach as fast as the river dolphin, who had now realized the danger and drove his tail down at a diagonal angle, swimming backward to get a good look at the hunted that had become the hunter. It took only one glance for the river dolphin to jump out of the water and do a complete twist, escaping with adrenaline boosted-speed.

The river dolphin didn't have any idea what this new creature was, but the razor-sharp teeth of his pursuer had given him enough of a hint of the threat that was posed. The animal was, in fact, a stray bull shark from the Atlantic, who had found his way into the twisting, turning rivers of the Amazon. Arguably the deadliest shark on earth, his stocky build and aggressive behavior made him a notoriously lethal predator. And the change of water type from the ocean to the rivers had no effect on him either, his only priority being to find prey to eat. Somehow, the river dolphin was still managing to evade him, even though the bull shark was bigger and quite a bit heavier.

While the dolphin's speed was giving him a sufficient lead, he would tire, and the slower bull shark would catch up with ease, so the river dolphin descended into a smaller, shallower stream off to the side. The bull shark tried to follow, ramming the bulk of his body forward, but for once, his heftiness was working against him. Seeming to give up, he turned around and swam away, letting the dolphin relax, but the bull shark whirled around and advanced at top speed. As confident as the river dolphin was in his plan, he did not have a death wish and fled, as the bull shark leaped clear out of the water to follow his quarry. From then, the river dolphin led the shark in circles and twists and turns, completely caught up in the moment and forgetting about the hunger that was gnawing at his stomach.

The bull shark was hungry too, but he did not want the energy spent in hunting to outweigh the energy he would gain by eating and eventually followed another tributary down to find something else to eat.

Even after the shark's retreat, the river dolphin was shaken with fear and only remembered his hunger after sensing a thin fish that he instinctively ensnared in his jaws. But that was all the fish he could find and, as he made his way back upriver, the river dolphin scrounged up some crabs that seemed to never be enough for him.

***

The loggers had hit a barrier, coming up at the edge of someone's land. Even if they illegally cut through it, like they had been doing so far, there were chances that the landowners would tell authorities, which was a risk they couldn't take. Daw had been sent to deal with the problem and he took two gunmen along with him.

Beyond a thicket of plants and trees was a small, ramshackle home that was crawling with vines. It was of a clay exterior, and the wood door at the front was crooked and unlocked, as the people living here did not know that they would have had to worry about trespassers.

Daw pounded on the door thrice, splintering parts of the dilapidated exterior.

"Open up!" he bellowed.

A man inside, wearing rags on filthy skin, looked startled as he came outside, looking for the source of the words.

"N- No, No English..." he managed to say, contorting his mouth to say what he thought was a garbled mess.

"Get me someone who speaks Brazilianese!" Daw commanded one of the gunmen and, now knowing that the people here did not understand English, proudly declared that the other should find any other person that lived there and hold them hostage.

Both of the people he had brought walked away, forced to oblige to Daw's orders, and one of them was shaking his head at his superior's stupidity.

"Daw, as an Amazonian logger, you ought to know that Brazilians speak Portuguese, or at least most of them. Regional native dialects are a whole other thing," he muttered as he reached the other workers. Raising his voice, he shouted, "Anyone speak Portuguese?"

Someone silently walked from a tree, leaving his chainsaw wedged inside its trunk, and followed the gunman back to Daw.

Meanwhile, the other gunman had located two children playing in the dirt at the back of the house.

"Don't say a word," He hissed in a low voice, but one of the kids, a little girl, opened her mouth to scream anyway. Not a sound escaped her as the gunman whacked his gun into her stomach and winded her before putting his grimy hands over her mouth and momentarily choking her because she could not retrieve her breath. The girl's brother watched in horror, but seemed to maintain a sensible state of mind, as he was slinking away into the forest, confident that he knew it well enough to get to his father and rescue his sister as fast as possible.

The gunman noticed that the boy had disappeared and drove his boot toward the little girl who was down on her knees. But Daw's angry face appeared in his mind and he knew that hostages would have to remain unharmed. Stopping his foot midswing, he resorted to kicking mud onto the girl instead. She tried to scream, but was so severely depleted of oxygen that the effort to breathe caused her pain. Clearly, what most considered to be the definition of unharmed was severely different from the gunman's quite relative interpretation.

Gripping her by the arm, the gunman dragged the girl's limp figure along the ground to the side of the house. The other gunman had arrived with a person who was conversing with the landowner.

"Tell him that our highest offer is $200 and he can keep his house and some land, but in return, we get to cut down trees in the area, and he doesn't tell anyone."

"I don't think they do dollars here, Daw..." the person acting as the translator said, exasperated.

"Well, figure it out," Daw snapped back.

So the person offered Daw's deal, which was worth much less than the land's true value, with Brazilian Real instead of American currency. As a result, the man refused, when, suddenly, from the trees, burst out a panting boy.

"Papai!" he exclaimed and told his father that the people were keeping the girl captive.

The other gunman took that as his cue to bring out the girl and hold her at gunpoint. Everything had worked out perfectly for Daw and he smiled with glee at his cunning.

"Wonderful," he said, "Everyone is here just in time for negotiations."

Stammering unintelligibly, the man agreed to take any offer if they just didn't harm his daughter or son. He even took the price that they gave, even though it was significantly below what he should have gotten for such a large piece of land. And he knew that, if he ever told anyone, he might come home from the market to find his kids astray on the floor, like his little girl was now, but worse. Dead.

All the loggers returned proud that they could continue to cut down trees in the area. But, to the landowner's terror, his daughter coughed up blood when the second gunman roughly dropped her to the ground like a ragdoll.

Chapter 27

"Daw '*Sawdust*' Miller," the former tour guide complained on the phone, "He's the one who ruined my business. That's the only reason I'm calling you, brother. Otherwise, I would leave you alone like promised."

"But that's the thing," the voice on the phone answered, "you promised."

"Please???" he begged. "And then I promise for real that I won't even utter a word to you again."

"Knowing you and your sorry excuse for a brain, that's another of your lies, but fine, I'll help you just this once. Just remember, the next time, I'll just chuck my phone off a cliff and leave it there."

"Yay! Thank you. Thank you. You are such a kind person."

"I'm not doing this for you," the former tour guide's brother cut him off, voice rising in pitch as he said, "I'm doing it for me and my sanity and my brain because you are the most annoying person on the planet!"

"I'll take that as a compliment," the former tour guide replied cheerfully. "So, how do I get started?"

"With all the empty land you have?" the voice on the phone scoffed, "It would be obvious to any person with a reasonable sense of existence. Preparing cattle for slaughter is your best bet. It's really successful and pays great if you know what you're doing. Break the rules a bit and burn into the forest to make more room for a feedlot. It's not like they will know anyway. And people are so dependent on eating animals that they won't even care."

"Okay. Thanks! Bye." He ended the call, relieved to stop acting cheerful and dumb to annoy his older brother.

"We'll see who ends up with the cash, *Sawdust*!" he sneered. He deposited the phone in its slot on the counter and proceeded to lay flat on the leather sofas designated for guests that would have been waiting in the lobby, imagining himself a world-renowned magnate of cattle ranching. The only problem was getting the cows.

***

Lucille was in a rage after the authorities had denied her of sending an investigation to the deforestation site. They claimed that the loggers had all the legal permits and were good people. She had argued that what they were doing was not right, but the people simply ignored her and also didn't believe that a jaguar had died where she claimed, even after she showed them all the bad reviews that the tour guide's company had gotten.

"We know a guy who presented his permit to our news channel anchor. It's all over the news. He's legal, and we can't just trespass onto his lawfully owned land. A jaguar's death could just be natural, and a good tour business will always hit bad patches. I'm sorry, miss," one had said, pretending to sound apologetic.

So now, Lucille felt as if she were out to prove the world wrong about her and save the Earth simultaneously, which was an overwhelming feeling, especially with the sadness that separating from her husband had incurred. But years of experience had taught her that she would get nowhere without a plan, so she set to making one.

"Well, first, I'll have to get more evidence because no one believes me and then... what?" she said to herself. "I can try to stop them single-handedly, get people to join my cause, or try to help the government see reason."

Lucille would not dream of choosing the last option after how the authorities had dismissed her and it was obvious which of the remaining two options she wanted to choose. However, as appealing as the idea of bringing down the loggers and tour guide alone sounded in theory, she saw reason and decided to educate as many as she could. After all, that plan of action would bring allies to her cause and give her a better chance of success.

Offering cash to a local for a car escort back to the jungle let her get back into action quickly, but guards stopped her before she could start heading toward the Amazon.

"Halt! Do you have permission to be here?" one person demanded.

"Of course. I have a permit for research here..." Lucille answered calmly, drawing out her phone to show a document, "and I'm sure that you can check with the people who have sent me here too."

"No, that's okay. We're just trying to make sure that the illegal logging in the rainforest decreases," Another of the guards answered.

"Aren't we all?" Lucille muttered sarcastically and the confused guards didn't come anywhere near realizing how close her remark was to the truth.

Chapter 28

The male monkey knew that the time had come to claim a troop, for if he didn't make his move while in his prime, the opportunity would never be in his favor. After contemplating when to explain this to his mate, he told her about his feelings while offering some berries. He received surprising positivity and support as the female monkey no longer wanted a lonesome life, even with the company of her partner. And she would also receive a high social status within the troop, leading smaller foraging parties when food was needed.

With their combined tracking skills, both monkeys quickly found nearby traces of a troop that had eaten in the area recently. The female groomed her mother once more before turning to leave and the mates raced in circles up a tree trunk, ready for a new life so that they could leave all their worries behind. However, from their spot in the tree canopy, the female could see the deforestation site and it had grown more than tenfold since the time she had first left to explore the human crane. The swaths of eroding soil, lined with death, were disgusting and humans were swarming the former homes of so many creatures. It was sickening how quickly a majestic wonder of nature was demolished by a race that was previously a part of the wilderness but sought to control what should be controlling it. The beauty of the forest was lost in the loggers' eyes and the monkey felt hopeless. But she tried to leave that feeling behind as she and her mate followed clues that hinted at the location of the other monkey troop.

The landscape was diverse, and the monkeys' movements varied with the trees, as they switched between fast, short swings and long, fluid ones. The excitement and anticipation became happiness as the two covered ground at a perfect pace, with nothing to bother them or slow their journey.

Something caught the male's eye, and he followed his mate as he descended a vine and landed in a puddle, splashing brown liquid around him. On the ground, he was vulnerable to predators, however, his arms were tense, ready to grab a tree and climb to safety. His lanky limbs also were bent at an angle and his tail stuck straight up. What he had seen was monkey scat and prowling a little further on the ground had revealed lots more of it. Then he heard the whoops and calls of his species, looking upward to find branches full of black-furred primates.

It was clear who the dominant monkey was, as only one was sunning in the center of the rest, being groomed by lower-ranking individuals of the troop. Now the female monkey was by the male's side and they both watched the troop's behavior. It would certainly be a daunting task for an attempt against this troop's highest-ranking member.

***

The grumble in his stomach was no longer the least of the river dolphins' problems. After the chase from the bull shark had left his energy depleted, food was his only salvation, but none was to be found. Now the pains in his stomach never got better and varied from minor nuisances to painful cramps throughout the day. A fish hadn't been sighted for a long time and fluctuations in the river level and speed made crustaceans harder to find, scattering those that were left farther downstream, into the unexplored. His recent experience had also made him more fearful, and he shied away from pursuing the possibility of food until he was absolutely certain.

The river dolphin's perpetual hunt for food continued even now, and the thought of competition had momentarily escaped his mind as he focused his senses on a miniature group of hiding piranhas that some luck had let him find. Small but full of sustenance, their distinctively shaped teeth and plump forms were partnered with the soft thudding sounds they emitted. It was not just their agility that the river dolphin was worried about, but their profound sense of hearing that could let them acoustically communicate his presence to the rest of the school, so he made sure he was very focused.

But his alertness didn't prepare him for the sneak attack of dolphins that snatched the piranhas away and left him with scraps he chased to the bottom of the river before it registered to him what had happened. The miserable river dolphin scraped up the mere morsels he was left with, before continuing down the murky stream to what he hoped would be food. But behind him, he heard the sounds of contentment as the pod of the other species of river dolphin enjoyed their meal as a family. Their chorus of chirps hit the river dolphin in a heart-wrenching way, as he reminisced about times when he, his sister, and the rest of his pod had acted the same way. This was when food had been plentiful, of course.

Though now, the other pod sounded as if they were jeering at his misfortune and all he saw was a group of bullies that were mocking his dismay. When he had first come to this part of the Amazon, they had rejected him and now he felt that their personalities were quite like humans: self-absorbed and cruel.

However, the other river dolphins meant no harm at all and had only stolen his kill out of dire need. Many of their members had been swept away by unexpected tides, exposed to the dangers of human civilization as they got closer to cities without any familial support. To preserve the lives of those that remained inside their pod, they had jumped at the opportunity for food. They had no idea of the river dolphin's tragic past and viewed him like an outsider.

The river dolphin proceeded to circle through tributaries of the river that branched out in all directions with a heavy heart. Fear and hunger had driven the thought of his family away for some while, but he should have known they would come to haunt him back eventually.

Chapter 29

Justin couldn't focus. His mind was blank and his stomach churned, until he felt like he was going to throw up. Lucille and her impulsive actions never were his kind of thing, but her personality had entranced him. Now his memories of her were only the sad ones, in which they had disagreements and arguments. From the outside, they seemed like the perfect match, however, Justin felt that he should have realized their relationship was bound to fail.

With his muscles tensed, his mind began working subconsciously and he began to pack up his belongings as if it were time to leave for another research location. He choked as he saw the photo of their wedding day that Lucille always kept with her strewn on the floor, interpreting it as a message from her instead of considering that it had been left behind in her rush.

Controlled by his emotions, he picked it up and dashed it against the wall again and again, until he suddenly collapsed into it, crying. It was more his body language that suggested it rather than any sound or tears. As a colleague walked in to see what had created the thumps on the wall, he saw Justin's shoulder's shaking and fists clenched. The person approached him, but Justin heard his footsteps from the doorway.

"*Get away from me!*" he shouted, clearly emotionally distraught. "You all... get... away... from..."

His voice died down as a second wave of emotions hit him and anger combated with sadness, both warriors wielding swords of regret. By now, the person from the main office had heard the shouting and had come to see what all the commotion was and found what he expected the least: Justin, the very same person who hated creating scenes and was always cool and calm, now slumped on the floor and still sobbing heavily.

Justin looked up at the newcomer with red eyes and asked wearily, "Why?"

Still in shock and confusion, the manager simply stared and opened his mouth before closing it again, just like the piranhas in the Amazon had done. That thought had occurred to Justin and now anger was back.

"I asked *why*. *Answer me*! Or do you hate me too, like everyone else?"

By then, the manager had noticed the packed suitcase and wondered aloud, "So are you leaving?"

"Yes, no... I don't know. I just— I quit! I don't want to be here anymore," Justin replied, still unable to calm down and maintain any degree of control over his rapidly changing feelings.

The manager looked taken aback by his reply.

"There are rules about this. You signed a contract."

But the retaliation was fierce. "Are there *rules* about *life*? I'm... I'm done."

So Justin, still in a state between depression, denial, and rage, stormed away in a similar fashion as Lucille, determined and not exactly sure what he planned to do, but with one major difference: his logic could not break through the wall of emotions that had built up in his mind.

***

It was a few hours until nightfall and the two monkeys were still learning about the troop's communication and organization. Soon, they approached and their uniqueness from the rest of the monkeys seemed to make them fit in. Upon closer inspection, every monkey in the troop was remarkably diverse in looks and personality, which made the two mates consider the possibility that they had found a group of monkeys who were more accepting of others. The troop's alpha would shoot the two occasional glances, but for the most part, seemed to be thoroughly enjoying his position. Through the misty dusk sky, the alpha seemed to be surrounded by an aura of regal mysticism and the two monkeys felt the need to respect him. For now, they resolved not to make a move and simply worked toward becoming genuine members of the troop.

The female introduced herself to other monkeys, as did the male and they went on short excursions on their own, bringing back small amounts of fruit that the troop could enjoy. It was relieving to have company after being alone for so long, boosting the spirits of both abandoned monkeys. Although many troop members still ignored them, others with more exuberant personalities welcomed them and treated them like family.

Among kinder members of the troop was another male who was grooming the alpha alongside others that were grooming the alpha's mate. He invited the male to assist him in his job and it felt somehow powerful to be serving such an essential monkey in the troop's dynamic.

As the male continued his role in grooming the alpha, with his newfound friend encouraging him in the process, he recounted how hostile his own troop had been to outsiders they had encountered when he was a child. Even when and if he outshone this troop's alpha, he decided, he would always be grateful for the welcoming culture that this troop followed. This group of monkeys had a unique social structure, which most other troops did not even consider, and it added credibility to the male's theory about it being, in part, made up of outsiders. His acquaintance introduced him to another of his close friends, who had recently arrived after being out to find food, talented in his foraging skills. They groomed each other and shared some fruits before the troop prepared for nighttime under the looming shadows of towering trees.

Chapter 30

The tour guide merrily sauntered out the front door of his cabin and admired its idyllic appearance. A solitary log cabin, amid the vast expanse of trees that provided the Amazon with its illustrious reputation. Then, he imagined the cows that he hoped would eventually find themselves at this very place. Barren land with the large beings slowly chewing their cud. He hoped to take ranching to another level. Another level of profit, of course, not sustainability. He imagined a few of his rare cattle without diseases slowly lumbering around an area with exhilarated tourists upon the brown saddles he would fit on the cows. Customers would look at the fine, premium quality genuine leather garments he would put on sale, from purses to shoes. A slaughterhouse painted with pictures of happy cartoon cows would mass-produce antibiotic-stuffed meat, and customers wouldn't have a clue otherwise. Labels like "grass-fed" and "humane" would greenwash consumers, making them all the more eager to increase the demand for his product.

But his imaginings of a perfect cattle ranch were interrupted by the sound of his phone, which he did not attend to until it ceased its ringing. He dialed the number back and engaged in a conversation with an evidently exhausted man.

"Please tell me you have an open spot for a job. I talked to every single place I could nearby and none of them wanted me after what I have been through," it responded, "I got your number from a manager you hired."

"A manager? Oh right, a manager. Never mind, "said the tour guide, taking advantage of what was probably a wrong number with his cheery tour guide voice. "I've got plenty of jobs and would love to have some new hands on deck! I'll send you the address and you'll soon have some work. But I don't think I caught your name."

"Oh, it's Justin. I've made some impulsive decisions in the past and need a new life. I just have to get away from my previous one. I'll be ready to work as soon as I arrive."

***

The pod of river dolphins was happy together, but one of their most social members was sulking amongst the outside of the group. She was the sister of the river dolphin who had regretted his escape and now it felt as if she had lost half of herself. Her brother was everything to her and after her narrow escape from the anaconda had come a despair-inducing revelation. Her parents tried to cushion the blow, for it was just as hard for them, but there was no easy way to take in the fact that her brother was gone. Immediately, she knew that he had run away in the danger, which greatly angered her, but at least she knew that he was safe and happy. However, traveling with her pod for a while had brought her upon an odd material in the water, similar to a fish but different in shape and feel.

There were multiple pieces of the substance, all covered in blood. Instinctively, the river dolphin could tell that it was the blood of her kin and sudden panic made her tail thrash in the water until her parents got her to calm down. They reasoned that there was no way to be sure whose blood it was, but she knew. And after more days of traveling in the same direction, she knew that in a desperate attempt to refind the pod, there was only one place her brother could have gone: the rapids.

To her, the rapids were a fabled place, full of sickening, heart-wrenching stories that elders of her pod told, followed by a drop into the abyss of the unknown. None of the pod members had ever been near, and it was just as well if the tales had been even close to true. However, another way existed to get to the bottom of wherever the rapids led. Unfortunately, it was dangerous too, even if the prospect seemed more appealing.

Caimans and large eels lurked among other river predators along the path she had considered, but it was the only way. If only she were brave enough. But for the time being, she had played it safe and convinced herself, like her parents, that her brother was fine.

However, more days soon passed and the sadness within her grew. She couldn't help but feel regretful for not going after her brother.

One night, safe with her pod, many older river dolphins had already retired, but the female river dolphin was awake in the gloom. Though her brother never left her mind, she tried to get rest during the night as well and fantasized about being bold for once and going to rescue him. Then her tiredness caught up to her and darkness swept her consciousness away.

***

At first light, Daw and his men were out and about, hacking at more trees and killing more wildlife, a lot of which was most certainly endangered. With the more trees that were cut, the more profit they made, so their greed for more kept increasing along with the amount of illegal deforestation taking place.

The burly men who would spend their entire day tirelessly piloting the huge, yellow and gray monsters that would destroy the forest, tree by tree, were early risers. They often poured themselves a large cup of coffee and, upon approval from their head, would commence continued destruction of the pristine land. Others wielded various tools like axes; they would dice the fallen logs into smaller pieces for easier transportation and sale. Among these workers were some who simply could not afford to live without the meager payment that the wealthy executives spared for them, and had to face constant bias that gave people like Daw more liberty and pay.

Above the noise of logging came a flurry of sharp cracks. A military field agent with a proud indigenous background stormed into the clearing with a gun. Bullets bounced off machines and embedded into wood, but they were only warning shots.

He advanced, shouting in English first and then Portuguese, "Everybody on the ground with your hands above your head. The people complied, fearful, but there had been preparation for this. Certain members of the team had been instructed to eliminate any authority figures that found out about them and, as the military officer started listing off the crimes that had been committed at the site, a single bullet blew his skull apart and he fell face first, dead before he hit the ground. Immediately, Gary started ordering people around. He had been the one to murder the intruder.

"People, get to burying him; he can't be found. And we have got to clean up that mess of blood and brain before somebody else comes along to accuse us of murder as well."

Then Gary treated the person's remains like he would any animal and trod on a piece of gray matter with his leather boots before spitting at the dead body and throwing his small gun to the ground.

A higher-ranking worker of the group emerged from the tents behind which he had been hiding with some of his fellow collaborators. They patted Gary on the back in a congratulatory manner and no one cared less about the life that had been lost for the sake of money and pride.

Chapter 31

Everyone Lucille had approached in the past day had better things to do and claimed to care for the environment as well, often while engaging in activities that harmed it. She didn't meet many people after the tourists near the edge of the protected areas of the Amazon and slept early in a tent, hoping for better luck the next day. Eating only a banana before getting to work, she trekked toward the last recorded location of the loggers. However, her phone had lost charge, making her rely on the sun as a compass.

It also took her longer than it could have because she was unable to follow a straight path consistently. Every bird call or rustle of leaves pulled her off course, beckoning with promises of living treasures. While she continued forward, a branch shook above her and she froze in an instant. Then, walking with very light steps, she edged around a tree and saw a giant snake forcing an unidentifiable animal down its throat. The lighting was perfect, and Lucille could capture the moment with a small handheld camera before noticing an insect near the base of the tree.

It was a praying mantis that was frozen in place, looking just like a leaf to anyone with untrained eyes. Waiting and watching, the green figure was impressively patient. As a flying insect veered closer, two front legs lashed out and ensnared the insect with sharp spines. The mantis ate the prey whole and assumed a static position once more, awing Lucille with power and skill.

Lucille had been watching for a while when a hummingbird swooped inches from her nose and captivated her eyes with a display of speed and grace as it went from flower to flower for nectar. Also on the flowers were a variety of native bees that were vital to maintaining the Amazon Rainforest's ecosystem.

After some time of chasing after a glimpse of wildlife, Lucille attempted to be more focused and covered more ground before resting on a fallen log. Now she was close enough to see some fires that burned at the deforestation site, but there was still a vast distance to cover. On the bright side, she still had most of the day to continue and planned to do so. But the fashion by which her husband had rushed in last time would not do much good this time around and Lucille planned to sneak in from another side. To accomplish that goal, she changed course and headed toward the river. It would make the journey longer, but hopefully more fruitful than it would be otherwise, despite the winding path she would take to see more wildlife would make her trip all the more lengthy.

***

Wanting to lash out and unleash rage at whatever was causing the loss of food, the river dolphin snapped its teeth in the water. After panic had constricted his brain, he didn't see the hydroelectric dam and failed to remember anything about it. Because of this, he couldn't realize what was making him starve and was not some unknown force. However, he had no proof of anything and, although the possibility of human influence on the biodiversity in his area had logically crossed his mind, there was not enough he had seen to support that besides his uncle's and the otter's death. And those didn't relate to food shortage; rather, they were the aftereffects of eating.

It all was a very confusing situation and there was no time to stop and think it through either. The river dolphin needed food, so he searched for it, but that, in turn, depleted his energy even more. Rarely, he was able to find some fish and, more often, various crustaceans, but what he was eating barely kept him alive and in a very feeble condition. While he was still young, he felt exhausted and dejected with his weary muscles, aching bones, a deprived stomach, and of course, no one to support him in any way. At this point, death was inevitable and the river dolphin knew it, but the only reason he let his starvation drag out for long and painful days and nights was the hope that, somehow, the humans didn't stop his pod from finding him. Then he would be at peace to pass, with his sister by his side.

It was terrible to see other family groups so happy as he had once been, but even they had their tragedies when humans took their own for trivial, unnecessary reasons. It made the Amazon seem like a trap more than a home with the colonization of such a destructive species. He felt that there was no hope and that it was better to accept that fact than to be disappointed time and time again to sink even deeper into his hole of depression.

Noticing a small monkey learning how to find fruit, the river dolphin remembered how his parents had taught him everything he knew, from finding to navigating the murky river waters, letting the water be a guide and not fighting against the current. But after the plastic had lodged itself into his mouth, causing scars that were still there, he had become frantic, not heeding his parents' warnings. And now he was in this predicament, separated from all whom he loved.

The sad, sluggish feeling made him sulk around, drifting with the current and his body went into a state of torpor to keep him alive. It may have been simple to just stop eating and let death come, but, while the occasional meal increased his hunger, the river dolphin was able to survive and keep on waiting for something to come. Not taking anything in his past for granted now, he searched for a sign; anything that could tell him about his sister and pod would bring immense relief. If they would ever meet, it would mean that his sister had befallen a similar fate to him and he did not wish that to happen, but even the reassurance that she knew both of them looked at the same moon when night fell would mean a lot.

Chapter 32

Around midday was the perfect time for the male to claim dominance of the monkey troop. He planned to do so in just one day. The two mates had assimilated well, but knew that it was better to act preemptively, so that their actions would not be betrayal, but a change in social organization for the monkeys. The male also knew it would be risky to take on such a knowledgeable and dynamic monkey, especially since none of the stronger males within the group were brave enough to do it. However, he would rely on intellect, for it was their kind's way to competitively decide dominance, to maintain order and justice within their ranks. The goal was never to kill and it was only somewhat about power.

If there were newer and better leaders with skills that won, it logically made sense for them to guide the rest. It was the same for subgroups of the troop that branched out to look for food and the male was confident that his mate would prove more than worthy for the position to lead those kinds of groups. And the entire ritual, where one monkey would be rejected from or assume dominance, relied utterly on intimidation so that no harm was truly done.

Tool use was commonplace among his kind and they often relied on dropping and shaking tree branches to scare away predators, so some of these strategies would surely be part of the male monkey's plan. His long limbs helped him accomplish the feat and he was able to use both his legs and hands to work on something, while holding on to an anchor with his amazingly strong tail. How he climbed through the trees with all his appendages truly was reminiscent of his namesake, especially because of his grace and speed.

Meanwhile, his mate was with a group of other monkeys, not wanting to get too close because she still felt guilty about her mother, but trying her best not to make those who were trying to make her welcome disappointed. Though close to the ground, they were also in the trees, grooming each other and simply lounging about. A few males were trying to impress them, latching their tails onto something before running along the ground with their hands and feet to go flying through the air. However, the females paid them no heed.

Before night fell, a group of monkeys invited the female along with them to forage and she felt internal pressure to accept, so as to not let them down. But it turned out to be a pleasurable experience, as they headed out to find food and returned as the moon was at its peak.

Upon returning, she found her mate and they curled up against each other, providing warmth against harsh winds from above.

***

"Alright, everyone, listen up!" blared a loudspeaker that woke every logger and every animal nearby. "A shipment of dynamite has been arranged so that we can pick up the pace here. We don't like to be kept waiting, so you must start working harder. Start today as soon as the dynamite arrives!"

A grumbling group of men was disoriented, awoken before the sun had even risen, but, even though dynamite could make the job easier, they saw dynamite as an opportunity for more pay.

"Hey! Why don't we get a raise for this? How 'bout that?" one person bellowed. "We do more work, you do give more cash, it's a win, win."

Someone else, presumably the one who had spoken from the loudspeaker, strode in front of the person who had shouted, puffing on a cigarette.

"How 'bout, if you don't want the money you are getting, you leave. We don't need you."

"Oh yeah? What if everyone here leaves? What will you do then? You need us."

"No, we don't. Along with the dynamite are coming people. People who will work free of charge. If you stay, double the work will get done and you might get more money. Improbable, but not impossible. If you leave, no loss to the business."

"But... that's illegal!"

"What legal stuff do we do here anyway?" the man said, spitting his cigarette at the other person's feet and strutting away.

Now in fear of losing their jobs, all the men simply waited until a flatbed truck rolled in. Containers of dynamite covered the center and grime-covered people sat along the sides, holding onto the boxes to not fall off. They were enslaved native people, brought to work, but paid nothing. It was more profitable to have expendable people working with the dynamite as the speed and rate of falling trees would increase. The job was already dangerous enough, a do-or-die living, but it was preferred to give the higher risk of it to the slaves. Hiding in tents would surely get the loggers kicked from the site, but striking the perfect balance between pretending to work and actually doing something was how most of the people planned to make the newcomers carry the heavier burden.

"Everyone get to work! There can be no mistakes because we only have a limited amount of dynamite. Use it well and we can get a week's work done in a matter of hours," the loudspeaker thundered, broadcasting a message again and repeating it in Portuguese after it spoke in English for the slaves that had arrived.

Chapter 33

The river dolphin's sister ate a fish that she had caught, while the pod kept following the river, with no place to stay hidden. They were approaching the place where she would be able to follow the rapids and the idea still seemed like madness to her, but there was no other choice. Because of the frenzy that the plastic bottle had driven her brother into, she felt empty and alone. Even if she died trying to reach her most loved family member, she would at least have some feeling of fulfillment in her life.

But the others in her pod couldn't know, because they would surely try to stop her, so she would have to distract them somehow. Her thoughts gravitated toward making them think there was a huge food source ahead, although she wasn't quite sure how to do that. And she immediately rejected the idea of tricking their sonar so that they would sense a nearby predator because of the stress that the memory of the anaconda still brought to many members of her pod. However, no deception was needed as, luckily, a current had pushed some crustaceans nearby.

While her pod was momentarily distracted, she made haste to flow through the roots of a half-submerged tree, facilely entering a tributary that would take her to the desired location like she was a river current herself.

The change in her surroundings was immediately noticeable. Foliage was thicker and vines reached down into the river like tentacles about to scoop her up out of the water. The shadowy mystique that came from overgrown trees was matched by an eerie absence of sound, making the river dolphin wonder if that was because of a terrifying beast that lurked nearby. So her body tensed up, and she moved slower in the water, trying to make less noise and movement.

It may have been her imagination, but sudden deep growls and sharp hisses that were emitted from beyond her vision sounded quite intimidating, with no indication of the sounds' sources.

For a moment, she wondered if all this was worth it and quickly corrected herself when she realized there was no option but to keep faith that her brother was out there. Somehow, somewhere.

***

Lucille had kept hiking and set up camp for the night, planning to go across the river the next day. Since the edge of the forest was the most obvious way anyone would enter the logger's place, she figured that approaching from another angle would give her more advantage. To do that, she would have to cross the river, which she was preparing to do.

Long nights previously had made her sleep in, but she was now as energized as ever. Her tent and other supplies were packed, but she was unsure of how to get across the wide breadth of the Amazon. She would probably get wet without a boat, but she couldn't just swim across because of all her belongings. Thinking back and forth about this gave her an idea. Justin had suggested it early before they had started their research trip.

It had seemed crazy at the time and still did, but Lucille had no choice. So she found a rope inside her pack and tied a firm knot on one side, securing it around a tree branch beside her. Then, she made another knot and flung it across the river. The first time, it came up short and the rope slapped the water before slowly sinking. After pulling it out, she tried again with no success, and the rope was only getting heavier from the water. Nearly giving up, she gave one more attempt, closing her eyes and flinging it toward the other side.

Through all this, a marmoset had been watching with interest and grabbed the rope from the air, just as it was about to smack the tree trunk. The monkey put it around a tree branch and poked it a few times with curiosity. When Lucille opened her eyes to look, the primate had vanished and she was quite astonished that she had managed to get the rope across with her eyes closed.

But that may have been the easy part. For, now, she had to cross.

She got on top and tried sliding across, but gravity brought her down to a dangling position. The jarring force from swinging to the bottom of the rope was almost enough to pry her strained fingers off, but she was able to wrap her legs around the rope to ease some body weight that her arms had to carry. Her actions gave her an entirely new view of the Amazon though it was impossible to tell whether it was terrifying, thrilling, or a unique mixture of both.

Inching across, Lucille roughly landed and fell against a tree, too exhausted to take any further action. Though the action would just so happen to come to her.

***

The male monkey knew that it was time. He had spent the rest of the day with others in the troop and now approached the leader. His intentions were clear and the two went through with the traditions and formalities before hooting and making an array of noises that attracted the attention of the others. Both competitors jumped around and tried to look more intimidating before the male took a daring move.

He quickly scaled a tree and shook its branches fiercely, making multiple sway at a time. The other monkey stomped on the ground, kicking up dust, and jumped onto a branch swinging back and forth.

As luck would have it, a downpour began at that exact moment and both monkeys returned to the ground with their tails raised. The fight would have continued, however, from the distance, came a familiar boom. All of the monkeys went for cover.

Everyone focused solely on the moment, leaving the previous conflict completely forgotten. Safety was the priority and there were no chances taken with the threat that the rain had set off. For, the notorious sandbox tree was like a predator itself, attacking all that came near.

The sandbox tree was large and covered in spines with green pumpkin-shaped fruits. Spines were followed by a toxic sap inside the tree and the fruit was spiny and poisonous too. Though, based on the behavior of the tree, one could almost call it venom. Because the seed dispersal of the tree resulted in the fruit falling to the ground and exploding. Parts of the fruit would fly everywhere for feet, with speeds greater than any animal in the forest could reach. And even the apex predators in the forest knew to stay wary of this creature.

However, the male had time to recover safely and he was disappointed in his failure. Besting the troop's leader was no easy task, but he had believed he was ready. Now he knew that a more experienced leader who could truly connect with all the monkeys was needed. His heart had no regret; he was satisfied with who he was.

Chapter 34

Floating by in the river was a branch that looked just like the one the river dolphin could remember so clearly. Of course, he had been playing with his sister, the only one he felt could truly understand him, and they grappled for the stick, full of joy. He didn't miss his parents out in this new world, but the one he shared such a close, unbreakable bond with had been separated from him. He was fearful that time apart would corrupt his mind and break the bond, resulting in his sister being crushed by his betrayal. He could see their reunion going wrong in so many ways because there was no chance of it happening. They had no idea where each other were and to survive without wanting to didn't work. He wondered every day whether he should give in to nature, as the bare amounts of food that he managed to scrape up decreased every day. Maybe it was a signal for him to just give up.

But it was not. The hydroelectric dam was now fully operational, making the environment a more unpredictable, unwieldy place, as opposed to the harmonious one it was before. It was, in fact, the humans' means of saving Earth that had nearly convinced him to nearly lay down his life. Less of this obstinate ignorance, that led humans to continue doing such projects as this hydroelectric dam around the world, was needed.

They would wonder if it was too much to ask, especially if better solutions cost a few thousand more dollars, but was it too much for the river dolphin to ask to see his sister once before perishing? The same question resounded in his mind as he absentmindedly chewed on a rock to keep away hunger. Yet, the architects of the dam would be celebrated as heroes, as the ones spearheading a change toward humanity coexisting with nature. And, in a way, they were. They were doing what they thought was right. But they didn't know how solving one thing would simply worsen another factor. It was necessary to comprehend that all of nature is interconnected. One thing alone could not be fixed. Over time, everything worsens in the presence of humans, and the ones to suffer are poor creatures like this river dolphin and even other humans who are oppressed and neglected by the rest of the greedy world.

***

The tour guide turned rancher had hired a few people to begin working, but he still didn't have what he needed to begin his cattle farm. The profit he had gotten from exploiting people on tours was enough, but his planning skills were far below superior and he had no idea what to do. The only reason that his workers were clearing the area and making it more suitable for farming was because one of them had suggested it. So the people were using the tools they had to get rid of the walkways, rocks, and other stuff, so that the soil would be devoid of anything but manure.

It took effort to hire, though, and that was the one thing the rancher wanted less of. So he decided to dump the work on one of his people. Time had taught him to give a little extra money and people would do just about everything.

"One of you," he barked, "Get over here!"

The man who came was Justin, who had become very grim and reclusive in his mind and manner. He strode over with large steps and his eyes were narrowed, partly from the work he was doing but mostly from all the glaring that he had become used to doing. His life was now purposeless and he only worked at this place since he had realized the killing of other beings made him feel better about himself. The job was for his satisfaction, instead of for money or success.

The rancher told him that he was to manage everything on the ranch, from the workers to getting cows for a raise that he might not want to talk about. The permanent scowl that Justin wore was almost replaced by a look of confusion, but he quickly recovered and nodded in agreement. As much as he doubted he would be capable of creating an entire cattle ranch, no other company was likely to accept a visitor to the country into their business.

Addressing the people wasting their time by just picking things out of the dirt, he raised his voice. "People! Stop dithering around and actually do something! We have enough materials around here to combine two of those empty buildings into a shed sort of thing. Figure it out. Get to work."

All the while, the rancher was relaxing and tapping away at dots on some phone game. This was the life for him. Lazing around while others did the work. All it took was a little money and some words here and there. He wondered why he had been a tour guide for so long when people were so eager to carry his burden for him. But it didn't cross his mind that Justin was only working for personal reasons and not out of the kindness of his heart. It was why all the workers slept on the barren wood floors of the empty tourist accommodations. And why they even listened to him at all.

Chapter 35

Hours had been spent tying the small red sticks of death to as many trees as possible, spaced out to maximize the amount of killing. One button would set them all off and if the people were not out of the forest by then, it would be their end as well.

"Last warning! All men out of the forest!" screamed the loudspeaker only once. To save time, the people would probably just set the dynamite off early because they didn't really care for the people. But to prevent some kind of uprising and to keep the people oppressed, they had to seem nice, at least by their standards.

The people rushing out of the trees like there were hot coals beneath their feet did not take one look back at the majestic wonder towering over them. The perfectly spaced leaves and the rough, sturdy bark, along with all of the animals that depended on those trees. At the base were the roots, surrounded by other plants only the Amazon had. It seemed too mighty to ever be defeated.

But the button was pushed and a single click led to resounding booms that were always followed by sickening cracks, and in every direction, trees fell, animals screamed in fear, and it looked like the world itself was collapsing. Gray smoke rose from the ground, suffocating those animals that were able to survive. All of the dense green environment was now only gray and gloomy. The entire area gave off the aura of doom, even if one chose to ignore the smells of death and sights of destruction.

It took a matter of minutes for the explosives to blow so many bases of the trees that would have taken days. Then the pollution entered the environment and would kill even more animals. Tiny animals within range of the explosion did not even have remnants and bigger ones' parts were strewn around. However, the loggers just looked on in awe, as if the demonstration of power was a beautiful sight. And just for good measure, a few even walked up to the wood to marvel at its demise. Or mock, depending on how one looks at it.

***

Lucille had been taking a break, sitting by the edge of the river, when she heard the explosives. The deafening noise made it sound like she was about to be crushed or blown to bits, but she was left alive, and feeling hollow, sensing the result of what had happened.

But all the while, as a silent tear trickled down her cheek, someone was watching her, ready to attack. To Lucille's credit, she only let out a small yelp of surprise when she rose and was met by a stick in front of her face. Though her surprise escaped her, the stick's welder showed no emotion.

She calculated that this was one of the Amazon's native people who was afraid of newcomers like her. Saying 'I come in peace' sounded too stereotypical to her and the man probably didn't know English anyway, so Lucille just raised her hands to show that she was harmless.

He understood the gesture, but did not want to be taken by surprise like when the loggers had blackmailed him with his children. So, he roughly shoved the stick between her shoulder blades, prodding her to his dwelling.

Lucille knew that if she could just get her phone, she might be able to get a few things across to this person, such as some pictures, at the very least. Depending on what she could do with the weak signal there must have been, she may even find a translator on the internet. However, her 'captor' was taking no chances, sharply tapping the stick at a point on her shoulder when she tried to reach for the phone in her pack, which made her arm go limp.

"But I need–" she began blurting, before realizing that it was no use.

The rest of the way was quiet, until what looked like a shack faded closer and closer into view. Two young children could be seen peering out of the back of the house with their hands covering faces through which peeked ever-inquisitive eyes.

The man grunted and led her inside the place. Feeling the pressure of the stick lessen, she started to turn, only to meet his arms shoving her shoulders into the wall. The exhaustion from crossing the river and now this; it was all too much. And, while she tried to keep herself conscious, there was nothing she could do to stop herself from drifting into black and collapsing in a heap to the ground.

***

One would have expected the male monkey to mope and wallow in self-pity after failing to take charge of the troop, however, the confrontation seemed ages ago with the new revelation that consumed all of his thoughts.

A baby monkey was on the way.

It had probably been so for a while, but they both knew that their child was coming soon.

Nothing had given him so much joy and the anticipation was almost too much. The male already knew that he would love his child more than anything, no matter what.

His mate was lounging in a tree and he brought her fruit to make her happy. With the news, he now did whatever little bit he could to make her more comfortable and at peace. She was just as excited for the coming member of their family, although it also felt overwhelming since she wasn't sure that she was up to the task. However, when she expressed her concerns to her mate, he reassured her by claiming she would be the best mother ever, even willing to sacrifice her life for her child.

But instead of making her feel better, this statement struck a heartstring and brought back the unhealed wound that her mother's death had created. She had never forgiven herself, even though the humans were to blame. With such anguished emotions already, the stress of bringing up a child was intensified, while she hung her head in sorrow.

The male, unsure of what he had done, remembered the awful remains of his mate's mother. She had been so grief-stricken at the time, but he had forgotten so easily. And for that, he chided himself harshly.

It was his sole responsibility to ensure his partner stayed positive but he had failed himself in doing that. Which made him wonder whether a baby was going to help or harm their life together.

Chapter 36

The river dolphin's sister had made it through the ominous tributary, but the rapids ahead looked even scarier. Unlike the path her brother had taken, there was no waterfall at the end. It was incredibly hazardous, nevertheless.

Water was churning in mini whirlpools, dragging sticks and other things underneath before dashing them on rocks and splaying them aside. The same had clearly been done to other animals, too, based on the limp remains of skin upon the jagged peaks of stone that protruded from the water.

She tried a different technique, entering the white water backward and swimming against it to slow herself. It worked, for the most part, until the water sped up and she was flipped over. Trying to right herself, the river dolphin's sister managed to get on her side, but the river would not allow further movement and forced her back down. There were obstructions everywhere and her echolocation was of no use with all the interference.

Writhing in the water, she had completely forgotten about the greatest and quite imminent threat.

The rocks.

In her struggle against the current, one found its way beneath her skin and sliced open her side. An angry channel of red poured out, getting into her eyes and mouth. It burned and stung and tasted very odd to the river dolphin, since she had only smelled something similar when her uncle had died from mercury poisoning.

As the rapids ended, she was flipped over and spun around, painfully smacking her tail into another rock, but what was on the other side was astonishing. Clear skies and waters with so much free life.

The animals were unafraid of humans coming in at any second and destroying everything.

She lifted her head above the water to take it all in, when a fish promptly smacked her in the face.

***

The river dolphin had sensed a fish nearby and was going to chase it, even though fatigue was growing so much that he could barely move. But then a fisherman's boat had come through the water and he had chosen to dive down and hide while the fish fled.

The one operating the boat had followed the same path as the fish, not to hunt it down, but to explore the area. But then, he had inexplicably cut the engines, as if to let something pass.

It headed back now, however, the river dolphin sensed something in front of it.

One of his kind.

Using the last of his depleted energy reserves, he quickly surfaced to swim closer, when the person from the boat shouted, "Bait!" and proceeded to shoot holes all the way down the newcomer's spine.

Mini fountains of blood shot up. Muscles were painfully ripped apart. Bones shattered into tiny pieces that punctured veins. The poison from the gun's bullets sank deep, contaminating the new river dolphin's lungs and insides.

It seemed to set off a chain reaction of death and pain that rocketed everywhere.

As life slowly seeped out of this river dolphin, she let out a cry of anguish, and then he knew. It was his sister.

With nothing left to live for, he stopped trying to sustain his already failing body and floated to his sister, where she saw him close his eyes and cease to live before the wounds in her body ended her own life, leaving the fisherman triumphant.

He had received twice the bait, meaning twice the deaths of fish. But the fisherman didn't see it that way. He saw it from an even more sinister perspective. To him, only money, profit, and personal gain came from the killings of these river dolphins. Their lives were a trivial matter.

***

Lucille woke up tied to a chair against the ground. Her bag lay in front of her and along with it was the man that had taken her. She opened her mouth to scream before realizing that there would probably be no one for miles around. So, instead, her attention turned toward getting loose and escaping whoever was holding her captive.

Expecting her to be awake, the man walked in with some water and roughly held it to her lips. With a look of bitter contempt, Lucille swallowed, not breaking eye contact for even a second.

The person who had tied her to the chair was none other than the same indigenous person whom Daw had blackmailed. Fear had taken root in his mind after how his daughter had been treated. Now, he could trust no foreigners and would take no chances. Whatever the consequences would be, he was sure that it would be better than his children being in danger.

The communication barrier between him and others made it difficult to make a decision about what to do with people that intruded on his property. Still, he was able to understand English, though he could not speak it, a fact that he made sure eluded Daw.

“Look, I’m here to help,” Lucille began, though she felt it was pointless. “The loggers haven't just hurt you. They have ruined so many lives throughout the rainforest.”

At the mention of them, the man’s face visibly paled and it certainly seemed that he was understanding what Lucille said. This prompted Lucille to ask if he could and he nodded in response, but then she also became aware that he could not speak it.

“So these people have hurt your family?”

The man nodded and held two fingers up.

“Twice? You mean you have seen others like them in the Amazon before?”

He nodded again and mimed eating something round, almost like a berry.

“Lychee? Guava? Um... Acai?”

Finally, she got a nod and now she knew how much more harm that people had done to the rainforest even before she had seen anything. Now, she had to earn this man’s trust and learn the truth about people exploiting the rainforest to confront the loggers and demand that they stop.

Chapter 37

The monkeys woke late in the day, feeling the heat of the sun beat down on them and the sticky air covering their bodies. It was a relief as the atmospheric rivers released precipitation down onto the forest; the rain quickly intensified from a slow pattering to a heavy downpour. As some used the opportunity to frolic and have fun, others looked for insects to chomp down or did other things for their enjoyment, but the male stood by his mate with his hand on her stomach and tail sticking up, alert. Over the past few days, her emotions had been going crazy, sometimes extremely gentle, while other times merciless and highly irritable. Through it all, he had stayed with her and was looking forward to spending the most exciting experience of their lives together.

Today, the female felt different, with less anticipation and more excitement. It was happening. She clamped onto her mate's hand tightly as the pink head came out first and the rest of its body followed. With tightly closed eyes, wrinkled skin, and patches of hair, the baby might have seemed like an eyesore to some, but to the proud parents, she was the most beautiful thing they had seen.

As if by the work of magic, the clouds parted above the three, casting a halo of light upon the family. From the rain and sun, the baby's fur glistened, while her mother held her tight, with a fierce determination to never let any harm fall upon her.

A gust of wind split rain droplets into mist and caused the little monkey's hair to stick up while she was curled up in her mother's arms, and her father decided that this officially made her the most adorable being the forest had ever witnessed.

While his parents were somewhere else in the forest, the female's mother was dead, but she knew that her mother was still watching over her, so she wanted to bring her child to her mother's body since she would not be able to present her newborn in real life. She basked in joy for now, but was mentally preparing to return to the edges of the forest again.

***

The hydroelectric dam was now fully operational and the entire team was quite proud that their efforts had paid off over the years, Jessica especially, in memory of her parents. She had dedicated her life in the hope that deaths like theirs would not be in vain and for all of the other young children who still had time with their parents.

Because the nearby areas didn't use much electricity, some small towns got one hundred percent of their energy from this dam, while the few bigger cities got a portion of theirs from this and the rest from burning fossil fuels. However, nearby, Dr. Jacobson noted the decrease in air pollution, which was also noticeable to the rest. It had not been perceived by any of the people before, though now that there was renewable-derived energy, they were able to tell what clean air truly felt like.

The Amazon, Lungs of the Earth, had long withstood human adulteration, but it existed solely for the beings within it, who took in some of the oxygen it gave them, while it took in the byproducts they released.

The atmospheric rivers seemed more like rivers as well, because the local water cycle was becoming less disrupted. However, the same did not go for the water itself. Not far from where the dam was, limp forms of animals were thrown onto the shore and the bottom of the food chain was evacuating the area. Predators higher up were left with diminished food and were forced to find new homes or resort to other methods.

All of this did not go unnoticed by the environmental scientist that Dr. Jacobson had talked to days before. He saw so much good and lots of bad as well. Unsure whether to reveal these findings, he knew that his ethical responsibility was to make sure of all plants' and animals' well-being. Then again, there was so much effort from the workers; they had toiled for months at the dam. And there were enough good impacts on the environment that it balanced out. Although he felt compelled to warn of the dam's dire effects, he stopped himself, speaking instead of how a magnanimous deed had been done for the forest and its animals.

***

It was another dreary afternoon, the sweltering heat of the Amazon bearing down on the workers who converted this tourist lodge into a fully functional ranch. The former tour guide bellowed orders from the comfort of a leather sofa placed on the verandah of the lodge. Rather than hold the construction tools that his dedicated workers wielded, he held a phone in one hand, sipping a strawberry daiquiri in the other, only caring to look up when the unpredictable internet decided to misbehave, or when his workers appeared famished. In the latter case, he would usually shame them by talking as if they were small children.

"I know you have it in you. You will be able to finish the job before lunch! If you can't, lunch will wait till you finish the job!" A sigh would be shared among several workers, who would then joke about their boss's growing paunch during his sedentary times, but their mouths would immediately snap shut when his irritable gaze rested upon them. Upon the turned head of the rancher, they continued their jests, trying to find some way to make the job less horrible. Most of them were destroying the entire land beneath them, pulling and hacking and ripping until only dirt remained. In places that seemed uneven, they would create small fires to make the work easier. It was all to make the feedlots where the cows would dwell until their time had come. And even the workers could tell how miserable living conditions would be. However, they had no other choice. This was the only job that would take them, and they needed the money. To them, it was either the cows or their families, what particularly prepared them to kill. The polluted air filled their lungs with ash and the destruction of the soil added carbon dioxide to the mix, preventing them from working with the efficiency that they once did. This was only worsened by the generous puffs from the rancher's fat cigar. From now, every day, every week, for months to come, this would be their lives.

Chapter 38

Coming to trust Lucille more, the man had untied her and let her sit comfortably. She made sure not to violate his trust in any way and came to understand how much the destruction of the Amazon had impacted him. According to him, others had been to the Amazon stealing acai from the wild and unsustainably farming it to sell in masses. Any of the animals that had come to the plantation were brutally refused sustenance. Just as this time, indigenous people had been blackmailed. Parts of his friends' and family's land had been stolen and put into ruin, leaving him alone with his children. The effects were devastating. It only benefited the corrupt business exploiting the land and animals. As they conquered more land for his microcosm of an empire, the number of animals that were killed grew as well. And the distribution of rare animal skins happened frequently. He narrated that every so often a rather invaluable animal would be found dead in realms of the farmers' land.

"Just like the leopard!" Lucille had blurted.

The man had not known of any leopard but did know of Daw and the kind of people he worked with, so it was likely to be true. In addition, word had been spread that one of the farmers had sold a single night monkey pelt at an auction for an unfathomable price of Brazilian real. Possibly even worse than that, slaves were kidnapped and used, who were none other than more indigenous people that also called the forest home.

***

Scattering bits of pink flesh into the swampy waters, the killer of the dolphins smiled, just from imagining how many fish he would be able to catch. The bloodstained pieces made small plonking sounds when they hit the water, leaching out a repulsive red fluid. But what were now just pieces of meat were once two living, sentient animals, though this made no difference to the ruthless ambitions of this fisher.

The first group of fish got caught in his net, adding to the red stains already in the water. Their fragile gills were trapped and shredded while the entwined threads dug deep into their skin. It did not take long for their eyes to roll back as death passed over. As the fisherman continued, he left breadcrumbs of discarded fish organs and brownish-red streaks in the water to attract even more prey. More waves of fish came, all getting tangled up in the ghost of a trap. The more he caught, the more he tarnished the natural beauty of the Amazon.

Slinging the overflowing net over his shoulder, dead fish occasionally plopped onto the forest floor, splattering juice onto the ground. But as long as he was making profit, how many fish were left decaying on the forest floor made no difference. Even if all were wasted, but he made lots of money off one, the deaths were worth it to him.

***

With surprising strength, the baby monkey clung to her mother's back as the two mates' arms oscillated through the treetops. They felt the wind in their hair, tickling their skin, while their feet skimmed leaves beneath them. Of course, the male's and female's prehensile tails were like third arms, instinctively wrapping around branches with minds of their own.

The male had wanted his mate to get over her traumatic past since he had first learned about it, so when she wanted to take her baby to her mother, he felt that it would provide a sense of closure and agreed. Though he would come to regret that decision very soon.

As the family swung through the trees, the baby made sounds of excitement. Her eyes were open now, deep, knowing spheres surrounded by a pink masquerade mask. Her fur was already growing in, sticking up in gray and black spikes.

As they approached, the deafening noise from the loggers grew louder, which was especially damaging for the baby. Her ears were not fully developed yet and exposure to sound pollution like this for prolonged time would create problems rooted deep in her physiology and psychology. However, the monkeys did not know this at all, adapted to living in a balanced environment, free of destructive humans.

It was clear how much of the land had been invaded, especially as the three monkeys got closer to the exposed, eroding dirt. At first, it had merely been a few square meters, but now, so much was destroyed. Because of the dynamite, lots more had been accomplished in a shorter time and, though none of them knew it yet, the mother's body had been vaporized in the blast.

At this point, they were practically at the edge between forest and destruction, trying to breathe in as little of the ash and soot as possible. As the loggers had removed so many trees, the natural air pollution filtering system of the area was essentially gutted. Thick clouds of smoke seemed to enter their fur, but the monkeys found temporary relief as they stayed closer to the ground, realizing that all of the filth was going upward. But to prevent any permanent lung damage, they would have to leave soon, just as the loggers should have, for their own sake, if nothing else.

Chapter 39

What Lucille had learned in a relatively small amount of time was stunning. The man had taught her about methods of life that people had abandoned, but benefited all of the Earth. Instead of commercial agriculture like the acai farmers, there needed to be a switch to regenerative plant farming, revitalizing the soil and pulling down carbon from the atmosphere. This, in turn, would sustain wildlife and create habitats that nature intended to exist. After he showed her these ways and how full of life the soil and plants could be, she recalled how great civilizations had fallen. It was commonly taught that unstable leadership and war were the primary destructors of ancient nations, however, most of history's first civilizations were long since enveloped in dust and dirt. The reason for this was rapid erosion, since there was not enough awareness about sustainable plant agriculture. But she didn't want her species to follow the mistakes that ancestors in the past had made.

This information along with other things just showed Lucille how much the native people of the land had to share, as well as the sad truth that they were undermined by some forms of media and other kinds of social oppression. It was just another dilemma that she would have to work toward changing.

After thanking the man for enlightening her, she did not know how to repay him other than removing the loggers from the Amazon, so that is what she went on to do. It was not far to the deforestation site and she came to a crossroads, both figuratively and literally. Taking a stand would change her life; of that, she was certain, but it was uncertain if she would have the right kind of impact. All Lucille knew was that there was not a powerful enough spokesperson for the repressed victims of environmental destruction, a vexation that had slowly continued hounding her until she was compelled to drive change.

So that is what she did.

Striding with such force and purpose that she was already gripping people around her, she called out to everyone, “We are all beings of this planet!”

Every head turned toward her, and she made eye contact with all of them, not backing down.

“Each individual that stands here today was born with the potential to do good, which can start at any point in life. What you have done up until this point can be put behind, and you can be better than the urging of our deeply rooted greed. This logging is destroying the habitat, homes, and lives of both people and animals alike. None of them deserve this treatment and are not doing anything against nature's whim, living in harmony with the Earth. Yet they are prey to this cruel, unsustainable “enterprise” of illegal logging. If not directly killed, their food supply is depleted, their lungs get filled with toxic air, or they have no place to call home. Ask yourself: is this really what you want to do to the one planet that sustains you? Killing off such a vital rainforest to the world’s health has serious repercussions that you may not even see. But you don’t have to see it to feel it. Deep down, I know that there is empathy, goodness in all of you. Your brains may see the money, but your hearts feel what is behind that. Rise above this!”

Now Lucille had her phone in her hand, showing to everyone the crimes of the loggers, the slaves, the burning fires, the lack of action from the authorities, and then the wonders. They were shown the animals and trees and sunlight that shone down on the soil and water. It seemed as if the grandeur of the Amazon of itself would bring salvation.

When Lucille blinked, it was over. A man had come out from behind his workers and, as if by an unspoken command, everyone went back to what they were doing. The man was accompanied by two others; they gripped her arms firmly, seeming to ignore her struggles.

The yellowing lips and teeth of the man that approached parted as he said, "Just what do you think you're trying to prove, miss?"

***

Lucille's captors took her inside a big tent and, quite ironically, she was tied to a chair once more. On her right was the exit, where light peeked through and she saw the forest border falling. Acting like it was a normal conversation, the man asked if she knew who he was, but she only answered with a shake of her head, glaring at him with pure contempt as she struggled against the ropes that bound her.

"I am the head of these loggers," he boasted. "I tell them what to do and they follow. We all make good money, the locals profit, and everyone wins, yet you barge in here and outrageously say that we should abandon our own property? If you haven't noticed, I'm trying to run a business here."

"It's an illegal scam!"

The man nodded his head toward her and a person beside him moved to gag her, muffling her angry shouts.

"Now, we wouldn't want to be talking out of turn, would we?" he sneered. "Outbursts like that are what get people killed out here."

As he finished the threat, movement outside the tent caught his eye and he mockingly gestured toward it. Lucille turned her head to look and was filled with despair, due to the family of monkeys that had come to the edge of the forest.

Their troop was not with them for reasons she didn't know, but that was probably for the best. Lucille could tell that this would not end well.

The monkeys descended, picking through leaf litter on the ground, looking for the mother's body. Almost positive that this was the exact place, there was some doubt in the mother's mind, but she knew they would be fine here, as the humans would not intentionally do them harm. The memory of the kind woman who had helped her when she needed it most was still fresh and the monkey was still misguided to believe that the loggers had not purposefully harmed her mother.

Lucille looked on, unable to do anything and the cutting of trees continued as usual. One of the men stepped near the monkeys and the baby, still learning to control her body, flopped near his shoes to see what the new object was. But the logger paid her no attention, simply continuing with his work and pushing his chainsaw farther and farther into the wood.

When the baby chirped, time seemed to slow down. Her mother turned her head to the child in utmost fear and Lucille was on the verge of tears, already coming to the unthinkable conclusion. The final slivers of wood were eaten up by hungry metal teeth and the massive tree plummeted to the ground, just as the baby monkey looked up toward it. Snapping out of her trance, the mother desperately ran for her while her mate already knew that it was too late. He looked away to lessen his grief, but the mother saw it all. Branches snapped as the tree came into contact with the forest floor and the cushion of leaves made it bounce up ever so slightly before resting on the ground, deathly still.

The baby never even had time to make a sound, she was crushed by the impact and the wood ripped her soft, new skin, swallowing her up. The female was too late, frantically trying to dig underneath the tree and this was when the male acted, for he felt there was hope left to save his mate. But, perhaps there never was hope at all, as this particular tree, as it had begun to naturally decay, was sentenced to death by a woodchipper.

The baby was already dead, but her mother clung desperately to the branches of the tree, willing her child to live. The male desperately cried out for her to return, but the pain was so much that nothing mattered other than getting her daughter back. Amidst these efforts, the wood was already being shoved into the wood chipper, sending bits of wood deep into the female's muscles. Still, she clung on, heartbroken and lost, until the realization struck to escape. The last thing the male monkey ever saw of her was pained eyes and her outstretched arms before her lower body was hacked into pieces and her eyes were never to be seen again.

His primal instincts finally kicked in and he retreated into the forest, also crushed, emotionally.

Chapter 40

Only silent tears had streamed down Lucille's face as she witnessed the tragedy. At the moment, she had been full of rage, but afterward, it seemed like there was nothing left except grief. She wondered why these particular loggers were so heartless, without a care for stewardship like most, but, of course, foresters were always better when they followed the proper restrictions.

Here, the authority could be just as bad as the offenders; she knew that. But she also knew it was no excuse. Dreading what was to come, Lucille struggled to stay awake as night came over the sky. But all that had happened in the day sapped her energy and a deep slumber was inevitable. Even as she slept, nightmares sabotaged her rest and gave her so much more pain because of the realization that the loggers were in power and could do anything they wanted at their whim.

In the morning, she awoke in a different place with a mounted jaguar head and eerily familiar pelt on the entrance of the tent. Looking into the big cat's eyes, she could still see the pain and, now, felt it. But those thoughts were cut off by a wheezing cough and boots that must have once been dark brown, now faded husks covered in a permanent patina of dirt.

Daw walked in, not quite making eye contact, but talking as if it was a normal conversation.

"If it were up to me, you would be our *prisoner* for much longer," he yammered, smiling much too gleefully at the thought of causing her more distress, "but the boss says we can't have hindrances in our work, like you. Personally, I don't think you'll be trying another stunt like the one you did anytime soon."

Lucille could clearly see that he was hinting at something that would have to do with her 'removal' and prepared for the worst.

Two of the logging goons, Lucille could think of no better word to describe people so gullible and morally inept, picked her up and roughly dropped the chair into the back of a tiny pickup truck and left while Daw simply smirked at her struggle, trying to get out of her bindings.

In mockery, he said, "Oh! Someone help me!" in an obviously forced high voice before his tone dropped several octaves, "No one is out there to save you and you will rot alone and helpless. Don't even bother calling for help."

The pickup was soon on its way into the forest, with Daw at the wheel, while Lucille desperately tried to center her balance and stop the chair from sliding around every time the car went over rough ground. And considering that they were in the "untamed" Amazon, all of the land was uneven. Whether it was for the better or worse, she did not know, but the chair was low enough that she would not fall over the sides of the truck. However, it did not make the utter helplessness any more bearable.

Picking a point in the sky to focus on was no help to ease her fear as the atmospheric rivers wove in and out of sight through the tree cover and the only fixed object within sight was one she could not bring herself to look at: the vehicle that was causing this suffering. And the ground offered no help, only sadness, as newly sprouting flowers and seedlings were crushed in the car's path, scaring some animals out of the way, but leaving frogs and insects twitching on the forest floor.

This drive was soon followed by something just as sinister; Daw left Lucille tied up in the woods without saying a word and had driven away.

Making the most out of the situation, she took in her surroundings, observing every detail, like the bolder animals that didn't conceal their presence as well as the more shy ones who came out of their hiding places for a few short instances. Even amongst all that had happened, nature offered serenity and perfect balance, allowing frantic minds to be at ease, even if that peace would only last for a short time.

***

Still not having left, almost the entire dam team marveled at the progress they had created in just under two decades. At first, all of the concrete and plant decay had released greenhouse gasses, but now they were able to offset that and much more. Jessica, too, was proud of the accomplishment, but was already pondering what other projects she could be a part of to help reverse the effects of climate change. Perhaps she would work in other areas of renewable resources or continue with the sustainable energy sector. Until she saw the change in the world, her purpose would not be fulfilled, or so she thought,. Although, this did make happiness harder for her, as it was only so often she saw the firsthand effects of her work.

Meanwhile, the churning of the water as it passed through the dam was such a calming, repetitive motion and she felt like relaxing, for once, to be in the moment. That tranquility was shattered, however, as a wild-haired, grime-covered creature stumbled into the clearing, rasping for water.

Jessica was one of the first ones there with a canteen of water in hand and a few others also rushed to help out whom they considered a mad person because they had been all alone, deep in the jungle.

After taking gulps of water and breathing deeply, the feral look of the one who had emerged from the forest was toned down. Seeming simply relieved to find other people, she began talking; the others soon learned that this "madwoman" was named Lucille and she had been held captive by a group of loggers. She told them about how they had murdered so many creatures and ruined the lives of people nearby and how she had slipped out of the ropes binding her to a chair, using her tracking skills to locate civilization.

Not being able to help feeling admiration for all that Lucille had been through, Jessica conversed with the newcomer a bit more and they were quick to bond. Both being passionate and having similar values made them connect deeply. Lucille was impressed with Jessica's work on the hydroelectric dam and Jessica, in turn, with Lucille's years of research. Naturally, with the twists and turns of their conversation, they ended up on the environment, sharing their approaches to conservation. Jessica believed in action-based environmentalism, while Lucille believed in advocacy more. But these two methods went hand in hand, benefitting their communication as Jessica began explaining how climate change was one of her top priorities. And when she expressed concern over the fish ending up along the riverbank and the impact on other wildlife populations, the other woman was quick to pass on the knowledge she had gained from the indigenous man about regenerative farming.

The emerging method of carbon sequestration was unknown to Jessica until this moment, but her ears were open, taking in the information avidly. Of course, she knew where food was sourced mattered and that lots of food directly caused deforestation, but what she didn't realize was that there was such a solution. The methods, the history, the benefits, all was shared, leaving Jessica stunned that an agricultural process to provide more food could also directly benefit the local ecosystem and global climate.

This time in talking had passed so quickly and it was already a couple of hours past midday. While the two had come together, others had wondered about what would happen with the random extra person who had shown up. However, Lucille knew that she needed to get back to the city and asked to be pointed in the right way. One of the people told her which direction led to a nearby tour guide's land. Figuring she should pay the tour guide a visit and find out what other exploits he had been a part of, she thanked everyone there and set off, now well prepared, on a trek toward what once was an area of tourist accommodations.

Chapter 41

Like it was right out of a classic cowboy movie, the sun beat down on the ground from overhead as it seemed to shimmer with the heat. All that was missing was the lone cry of a hawk looking for food. The only contrast from the barren land was metal bars trapping large lumps, forced so closely together that there was little room to move. Even if it were possible to walk around, the action would have been pointless.

This was the former tour guide's feedlot; the helpless animals within were his cows. The poor ruminants were being fattened up with an utterly malnutritious diet of wheat and corn that kept them just a hair away from the brink of death. Many of them had never even touched an open pasture in their life and it was now certain that they were never going to. Aside from the food, their bodies were full of antibiotics and hormones, both force-fed and pumped into them, maximizing meat production without any care for well-being. Most of the cows within this cruel enclosure had some kind of disease, whether it was chronic or not; the pain was felt internally and externally. And their bodies were covered in urine and feces, with no other way to relieve themselves. The amount that could be salvaged was dumped into a part of the Amazon River nearby, which the same water source used for the cows.

Many of the workers here, such as Justin, felt that killing was the solution to dealing with their emotions. However, those hired by the "rancher" were also forced to endure the choking air and rancid odor that rose from the feculent land upon which the cows lived. There were alternatives to farming like this, but they cost more and produced less meat. What mattered here was the money, not the morality. However, unnecessary killing cannot be morally justified, even when some aspects of treatment may be better than standard practice.

After other stages of cruel torture, this and other feedlots were the final places the cows came before their slaughter. Seeing it all from within the forest, Lucille could not believe that this was how much of her food was sourced. Of course, she had known the act of killing was cruel, but all of the torture that came before it was new to her. Before, her justification had been that humans were supposed to eat meat, but she knew this should not be happening. The revelation seemed to be the final straw; something, perhaps her sanity, cracked deep within Lucille, and the real world faded out.

In her mind's eye, she saw the cows disappearing, blood and flesh left in their wake. Then the forest, burning to the ground, crushing animals as they already were dying. The vivid vision showed a resource-depleted forest that continued to be exploited by humanity. Everything seemed so hopeless.

Feeling both horrorstruck and betrayed, all of the emotions that Lucille had been holding back, in the hope that something would come out of her journey, came out, and she collapsed onto her hands and knees. The sticks and stones piercing her skin were ignored as the pain was nothing compared to what she felt inside of herself. Her breaths came out short and rapidly while her mind seemed to be shutting down, bit by bit, leaving her shaking her head from side to side like a puppet. Sitting back on her knees, Lucille let her head limply drop into her arms and was heartbroken that she could not have stopped corruption and evil like what she had seen. If only there was less greed and more logic, more awareness of the truth, and more drive toward change. But she had tried following that path and it had taken her nowhere. She was left half-mad and depressed, with no feeling of worth on the planet. She wished that she could be understood. She wished that she could have accomplished her goals. She wished that someone, something, *anything* could have a voice. A voice for nature.

Epilogue

Far beyond the logging site, even past where the river dolphin had ended up before his death, droplets of water came down from the freshly replenished atmospheric rivers. No humans tread on the land here, but it was isolated from the rest of the Amazon due to modern development. Neither human nor animal went out of their respective territories, for there was an unspoken agreement between the two, leaving the area free to thrive as an oasis amidst a desert of despair and destruction. Many major tributaries flowed into this land and there were a few small ones that sometimes entered as polluted water, but exited being clean and pristine. It was the same with air entering the trees, quickly cleansed of its contaminants.

Here, another jaguar prowled in the forest, able to sustain himself because of a stable wildlife population. Hunters were practically unknown to him and finding a mate was his worry, not finding a gun pointed at his head. Multiple monkey families could swing in the trees, enjoying each others' company instead of worrying if the next day would be their last. Fruit was plentiful, letting them satiate themselves and increase biodiversity in the forest. While no river dolphins lived directly in this area of jungle, the variety of fish here surpassed that found in other places of the Amazon River and the pods of dolphins lived in harmony further downstream, finding no reason to quarrel. Their nourishment was not unpredictable, leaving them to socialize and develop close bonds that could last a lifetime.

Other animals flourished here, too, able to call the treetop canopy and other parts of the forest their home. Because, without harmful human activity, nature sustains itself in an endless, regenerative cycle. It is only when that cycle is broken, that problems are created, eventually reverberating across the globe. The natural world just needs a slight push from the people who did it wrong, to set it back on the right path. People who are doing this have helped in holding the planet on the brink for now. But lives are left to save.

Author's Note

Just a few years ago, when I was in 7th grade, I began to truly explore my passion for creative writing. At the same time, there was a growing urge within me to make my voice one that could stand up for nature. And luckily, these two went hand in hand. I dreamt of nature often, but knew, at the same time, how imperiled it was. Yet, when I first began my writing, I had no idea this is where it would end up. Every waking moment I continue to think of the plight countless animals are in, as a result of humanity's destructive desires and truly wish for more to share their voices, so that, together, we may shield our planet from the harm that is yet to come.

It may seem cliche that I chose a location like the Amazon Rainforest, with my primary characters being animals that are typically well-known: a jaguar, monkey, and river dolphin, but this was simply so that readers would not feel detached from the story. I wanted this to be about their experiences, which would not have been possible if it was necessary to provide a scientific understanding of everything I wrote. Of course, in this process, I learned as much as I could about what was included in the story. Over these years, I have also discovered that, not just writing a story, but turning that written work into a book is something that requires much perseverance and dedication. For that, I sincerely thank all of my readers, who make every moment worth it.

One more thing that I feel I should add is some elaboration on the title of this work. When thinking of a title, I wanted to capture the essence of my message while having meaning as a standalone phrase. *Auctioning off Existence* means exactly what it seems: humans are selling off the existence of all living things to the highest bidder.

Please remember, this story is not yet over: These animals may have died, the villains might have won the day, and our hero may have lost, but it is each individual's moral responsibility to finish what she started. While the characters in this story may have been fictional, environmental destruction, social injustice, and animal cruelty are all major problems in our world. Real lives are taken every day. Pristine, untouched nature is being invaded and attacked. Marginalized populations are being affected. And something needs to be done.

Acknowledgements

Firstly, I would like to extend my thanks to someone who this book would not have been the same without - my amazing friend Ishaan Gaikwad. From the time in middle school when I was only beginning to formulate ideas, to its final stages, he was with me every step of the way. Especially during the Covid-19 pandemic, our collaboration allowed the story to flourish into so much more. For that, I am extremely grateful and truly believe that I would not have gotten here without his incredible support and friendship.

I also wish to express my appreciation for my exceptional 7th grade English teacher, Ms. Lyndee Kim. In her class, I was given the opportunity to explore what creating a story truly meant, which is something that I have never otherwise experienced in a school setting. Simply having the freedom to write motivated me to pursue the creation of a book.

Finally, I must acknowledge countless friends who gave me inspiration, as well as my parents and sister for their support in this process.

About the Author

Aashay Mody has been fascinated by natural beauty for as long as he can remember, inspiring him to start his debut novel *Auctioning Off Existence: The Tragedy of the Amazon Rainforest* in 7th grade. Since going vegan at the age of 12, he has strived to benefit nature by making numerous changes in his life. Aashay hopes to encourage preservation of the environment and believes all beings on this Earth are worthy of living. Other than pondering the fallacy of human superiority, you can find him out birding, reading a good story, or enjoying classical music.

www.ingramcontent.com/pod-product-compliance
Ingram Content Group UK Ltd.
Pitfield, Milton Keynes, MK11 3LW, UK
UKHW041638190726
13854UKWH00006B/2572